BARRONSGATE

BY
DENISE ST. YORRE

To Clifford & Sally
With Love,

Becca
("Denise St. Yorre")

PublishAmerica
Baltimore

© 2003 by Rebecca Babcock.

First printing

ISBN: 1-4137-0773-4
PUBLISHED BY PUBLISHAMERICA BOOK PUBLISHERS
www.publishamerica.com
Baltimore

Printed in the United States of America

To Trent,
For your patience and your sense of humour.

ONE

The flickering firelight danced in the reflection on the window panes, as though wishing away the cool darkness outside. Inside, Marianne walked slowly to the full-length mirror, feeling suddenly like a princess. She was pleased as she examined her reflection in the wide glass. The mirror, like the room, had been her mother's; Marianne seldom used either. Tonight, however, she had allowed her maid to coax her into the spacious chamber in order to don the new plum-coloured dress that her father had purchased for her in London the preceding winter. She was unaccustomed to dressing in such fine clothes, but could not help admiring the effect. Sarah, her maid, had piled Marianne's dark hair becomingly onto her head, and the deep purple colour of the dress set off her fine, fair skin on her bare collarbones and delicate features. A rush of excitement for the evening brought a deep glow to her cheeks and full lips. She turned her head side to side, surprised and delighted by the reflection that greeted her in the glass.

"You look lovely, Miss," Sarah said, beaming with pride. Marianne smiled at her with a mixture of wryness and pleasure. Most evenings, Marianne was most likely to be found by the fire in her father's study, reading one of the thick volumes from the shelf, or discussing the contents with him. She was likely to have dirt under her nails from helping the gardener in the rose garden, or deep purple stains from the blackberry bushes that grew along the lane. Tonight, however, she had coaxed her dark, unruly hair into a becoming twist upon her head, and had donned the luxurious silk dress at her father's request. She had shielded her reluctance from him in her desire to please her closest, and indeed, only companion.

"You are too seldom in company," he had told her only a week ago. "And the Captain is your brother's dear friend." Privately,

5

Marianne had believed this to mean that the Captain was an unruly, unmanageable individual, but she had rather dance a thousand times with such a man than to hurt her father by saying so.

"It would make me very happy to meet him, then, Father," she had said, smiling.

"Good girl," her father replied, his eyes – still so much like her own – crinkling sympathetically. Then he returned his attention to his book, content and comfortable as his daughter watched him.

Marianne smiled at this thought, and she walked to the delicate wood dressing table, which was now a little old-fashioned, but still beautiful. Sarah left the room, still beaming, and Marianne blew out the candle and crossed the room, closing the door behind her. She walked down the short hallway that led from the main stairs to the family bedrooms, then started slowly down the stairs, careful not to step on the hem of her gown. "Father," she called. "I am ready."

He emerged from his study, and smiled as he saw her, reaching out his hand in greeting. "Come, dear," he said. "The carriage is ready – we mustn't be late."

"What?" Marianne teased. "Not surprised to see me looking so fine?"

"Not a bit. You are always beautiful, my dear." He held out his daughter's cloak for her, then drew it tightly around her shoulders.

"Of course!" she replied, laughing, but inwardly pleased at her father's compliment. "And each guest tonight must, of course, agree with you!"

"Oh, but they will," the dignified older man replied, steering her through the front hall and out the door. "Only you haven't been out in the world nearly enough. You will see, everyone will love you as I do."

Marianne laughed, breathing in the still-cool early summer air. "I only hope that you are right. Of course, since you are wrong so seldom...."

"Never, never!" her father cried, helping her into the carriage. "I am never wrong, my dear. And you will see how everyone loves you. How can they do otherwise?"

"How, indeed?" she replied with mock-solemnity as the carriage lurched down the lane.

6

The neighbourhood of Barronsgate, the Reed estate, was a quiet one nestled among apple orchards and sheep farms in Kent in Southeast England. It had been little disturbed by the recent wars against the French and Bonaparte; indeed, it is very possible that many of the farmers, most of whom were Mr Reed's tenants, were not aware that a man named Napoleon Bonaparte existed at all. Marianne loved the quiet and seclusion of her neighbourhood, and had little desire to ever leave it. The entertainments of London and Brighton held little allure to her, compared to her quiet, comfortable home, the lovely countryside, and the company of her kind, elderly father.

Into this neighbourhood Captain Philip Weston had recently arrived. He had moved into Trent Cottage, a charming place only a short distance from Barronsgate. As they rode there in her father's carriage, Marianne wondered about this friend of her brother's, and why he would choose such a quiet, unfashionable place to make his home in. She could not imagine that her brother would associate with anyone who was seriously attracted to quiet country life.

Edmond Reed was nearly ten years older than his sister, and Marianne remembered him only as an unmanageable young man who had once caused her parents so much worry so many years ago. His disposition was entirely unlike Marianne's, and he had been only too happy to leave the simple seclusion of country life. Five years earlier, he had failed to come home from his trip abroad to attend Mrs Reed's funeral; since then, Marianne had been unable to hear his name mentioned without a shiver of animosity. Knowing how selfish and unreliable Edmond was, Marianne could not believe that he had been able to attract any friends worth knowing. Her father, however, had been inclined to forgive his son his wrongs since the death of Mrs Reed. Marianne, for her part, believed that Edmond's continued absence allowed this state of grace and forgiveness to endure.

As the carriage approached the small, elegant home, Marianne allowed herself a subtle flush of pleasure. Trent Cottage was a place that she had passed many times, and that she had always wished to enter. It was a charming building, but had been unoccupied since Marianne was a young child; its owner had built it after his move to Kent from Nottingham, and lived there only a few years before he

7

and his family settled permanently in London. At first, they had used the cottage as a country retreat, but by the time Marianne was a young woman, the family had lost interest in the quaint little home. Consequently, the inquisitive Miss Reed had never been able to explore its rooms. Now, despite her distaste for the company of her brother's friend, she was eager to see the inside of the place that had charmed her since she was a child.

Mr Reed and his daughter were met at the door by a demure servant, and were then led into a spacious, but warm chamber at the front of the house. Their names were announced, and Marianne noticed with pleasure that several other families of the neighbourhood were in attendance. *At least we won't be alone with Captain Weston,* she thought. As she smiled and greeted her father's friends and their families, she admired the graceful room, with its slightly old-fashioned furniture, the warm, invitingly coloured fabrics, the subtle, fine touches of elegance throughout. She was appreciating the delicate stitching on a footstool near the fire, when Captain Weston entered the room. He was a handsome, well-built man, with thick, dark hair, and light, intelligent eyes. He moved about with a grace and elasticity that drew his guests towards him like moths to a flame. He was a handsome, charismatic, charming man, and Marianne disliked him instantly and intensely. Reluctantly, she stood and moved to her father's side, a polite smile barely curving her full lips. She watched Captain Weston move about the room, greeting his guests, charming them with his wit and manners. She watched as mothers eagerly introduced their eldest and prettiest daughters, as gentlemen suggested shooting expeditions and dinners. She could not help but smile as her neighbours the Farthingtons pressed their eldest daughter upon him. Charlotte Farthington was only a few years older than Marianne, but it was well-known in the neighbourhood that her parents already despaired of their daughter ever marrying. For a moment, Marianne was amused by this magnetic quality that Weston possessed. Then she remembered her own brother's charm and ease with company, and fought to ignore the scorn and mistrust that suddenly threatened to stifle her.

"Backward man," she whispered ill-naturedly to her father, "he should have met his guests at the door."

"Hush, my dear," Mr Reed whispered as their enigmatic host approached them.

Finally, Weston was before her father, his light, intense eyes focused intently on Mr Reed's face.

"Mr Reed!" he said, his voice at once controlled and eager. "It has been many years since I have seen you, sir."

"And then only once. Welcome to our neighbourhood, Captain." Mr Reed greeted Weston warmly, grasping his hand and smiling.

"I thank you." Weston nodded politely, his eyes focused upon the old gentleman's face. "And this, I presume, is your daughter?"

"Yes," Mr Reed replied proudly. "Captain Weston, this is Marianne Reed."

Weston turned to Marianne, and she was, for a moment, startled by the intensity of his pale grey eyes. His gaze seemed to eliminate everyone else from the room, to absorb her entirely. Her chest contracted and a feeling of warmth and unease uncurled itself in her stomach. She noticed the fullness of his lips, the curve of his slight smile, but without disengaging her own eyes from his. She offered her hand, felt it in the cool strength of his own fingers, and wondered whether this was not a rather long moment for her own hand to be within his, so. And yet she did not pull it away.

"And this must be Mrs Weston." Her father's voice startled Marianne, and she snapped her hand back to her side before she was even aware of what he had said. She had not noticed the slight, delicate-looking woman approach them. Captain Weston turned to her, and Marianne believed that she saw his eyes darken in annoyance and hostility.

"Mr Reed, Miss Reed," he said, "this is Louisa Weston." His voice was as calm and level as before, but his eyes had lost their engaging warmth. Immediately, Marianne felt a warmth and sympathy to this gentle, unassuming woman. *What a brute her husband must be*, she thought. She reached out her hand and took the other woman's cool, thin fingers in her own.

"I am very glad to meet you," she said. "We see so few people in our neighbourhood. I hope we shall be friends." Mrs Weston pulled her hand away, looking shyly at the floor, refusing to meet Marianne's eyes.

"But I see that you have many neighbours," Captain Weston replied, amused.

"Yes, that is very true," said Mr Reed. "But we see them so seldom. You see, Trent Cottage is closer to Barronsgate than any other house in our neighbourhood. We are very glad to have such old friends so close to us now."

"Yes," Weston replied, an electric light in his strangely pale eyes. "It is good to be near such old friends."

Mrs Weston turned then, her gaze still upon the ground. Marianne again felt a twinge of pity for this strange, shy woman, who was hardly more than a girl. Her husband, however, took her by the arm, his grasp firm, but not rough. "No, Louisa," he said. "Our other guests are well occupied. Please stay and entertain Miss Reed." Marianne's cheeks flushed hot with anger at the domineering Captain. Louisa Weston stepped forward obediently, and led her guest to a pair of chairs near the fire without ever speaking a single word. Marianne sat down, wanting to draw the reserved young wife out of her shell.

"I am afraid that my brother has shared very little with my father and me about your husband. I did not even know that the Captain was married. Are you far from home?" she asked.

"Yes, very." Mrs Weston was staring steadily into her lap, but her cheeks had taken on a little colour by the fire. Marianne wondered what to ask next.

"You must miss your family, then."

"No-yes. That is, I can no longer...."

Instantly, Marianne's pity for this young woman intensified. "I understand," she replied quietly.

"I don't think you do." Louisa's voice was almost angry.

"My own mother died when I was nineteen," Marianne continued softly, tears springing to her eyes. "I still miss her a great deal." The tiny woman remained silent, her face turned away from Marianne's. There was a long silence, and Marianne felt an intense sympathy for Captain Weston's wife. *What a life she must lead*, she thought, *with that man her only friend!*

Soon, Mrs Weston was called to meet her other guests, and Marianne, to greet her father's friends. She stood at Mr Reed's side, smiling and assenting, but without really paying attention to the conversation. She was watching the Westons circle the room. Captain Weston seemed almost to have to lead his wife about, and she seemed almost unwilling to follow. Her shyness made her slightly awkward, and Marianne wanted to rush over and break her free of her husband's grasp, to lead her to a quiet chair near the fire where she would not need to play the hostess, to laugh and accept invitations and remember names. Marianne was so absorbed in Mrs Weston's unease that she was shocked to discover, her attention suddenly diverted, that Mrs Weston's husband was watching her! Indignation and self-consciousness were delayed as she was once again caught in the pull of his grey, magnetic eyes. She was unable to pull her gaze away, and she watched as his full, masculine lips curved into a knowing smile. His eyes glinted with assured confidence.

Her father's voice once again withdrew her from their depths, and she turned to answer him, drawn once again into an unengaging conversation about the new pastor in a nearby parish, but she could still feel Weston's eyes on her. Her cheeks flushed with colour, and her ears rang. She wished to walk over to him and slap him, to make him feel the sting of his own rudeness. She wished to brush the feeling of his gaze off her skin. And then, languidly, he moved towards her. She felt, more than saw his approach. Marianne turned in confusion, only to discover that her father had left her side. She was to speak to this impudent Captain Weston on her own!

"I see that you have freed yourself from Louisa," he said, a cool smile pulling at his lips. "I hope you have not found her company tedious."

"Not at all," Marianne replied, her voice light and controlled. How she wished to walk away, to join her father near the window! "We were having a very pleasant conversation. But her other guests required her company as well."

"Oh, I am sure that none of these guests are half so interesting as you are."

Marianne's chest tightened. How was she to reply to such a remark? His strange, cool eyes were almost dancing, drawing her into this strange game of his. With difficulty, she smiled. "I am

11

flattered, Captain, but I am sure that you praise me too highly."

"Who spoke of praise, Miss Reed? Perhaps you are interesting in a manner not worthy of praise."

What game is he playing? Marianne fought to maintain her composure. His strange manner and obscure comments made her feel like fleeing, not only to her father's side, but to her own home, to her own bed, away from Captain Weston and Trent Cottage. But she was unable to pull her own gaze from his dark, handsome face, from his magnetic eyes. "What do you mean, sir?" she finally asked, her voice shrill and tense to her own ears.

Slowly, fluidly, Weston leaned towards Marianne, and she had to tense herself from either pulling away rudely, or worse, from leaning in towards him. "Are all interesting young women chaste, Marianne?" he whispered, his breath brushing her ear, the hairs on her cheek. Marianne's mouth went dry.

"Pardon me, sir?" she asked hoarsely, understanding his question, and yet unable to formulate a reply.

"It seems to me," he replied, standing straight once more, his voice calm and level, "that vice is often more interesting than virtue." He spoke as though he were discussing the price of linen in London. His calm assurance shocked Marianne.

Instantly, she recovered her wits. Her temper flared, and she had to restrain herself from striking him, from flying at him in her rage. "In that case, Captain, I am very sure that I am not interesting at all – not in the manner you suggest."

"No?"

"No, sir, I am not. And I wonder how you would react if someone were to suggest of your wife what you have dared to suggest of me."

Captain Weston's light, playful countenance darkened, and Marianne regretted her hasty words. "Be careful what you say of Louisa, Marianne," he said, his voice low and threatening like thunder in the distance.

"You are quite right, sir. Mrs Weston did not deserve such cruelty. But I assure you, sir, nor do I. And I have not given you permission to use my Christian name, *Captain* Weston." She turned sharply, and strode across the room to meet her father, fearful of losing her temper once again.

Marianne and her father did not leave before Captain Weston had promised that his wife would call on Marianne the following day. Mr Reed was delighted, and even his daughter was pleased at the thought of this visit, though she could not share in his wish that her husband could accompany Mrs Weston on her visit.

"We are very lucky to have such fine neighbours," he commented in the carriage as they rode towards home. "Especially as Trent Cottage has been vacant so long."

"Yes," Marianne replied, trying to keep her voice from becoming as grim as she herself felt. "I am sure that there are not two other such people in the world as Captain and Mrs Weston."

Marianne rose early the following morning, eager for her new acquaintance's visit. She felt sorry for the shy, reserved woman, but what was more, she liked her. Even in their brief, somewhat strained conversation, Marianne had sensed in Louisa Weston a strong and impulsive spirit – something that Marianne admired. She disliked people that were too calculating, too much without feeling. She felt that such people were seldom worth knowing, as there was rarely anything to discover in their characters, rarely anything below the surface. She was certain that this was not the case with Mrs Weston.

Her visitor arrived not long after lunch; her husband's gig dropped her off at the front doors of Barronsgate. Marianne was surprised that Mrs Weston had not walked or ridden; their two homes were so close together, and Marianne herself often found it a pleasant afternoon stroll. *But she is such a delicate thing*, she realised, *she must be too weak to walk so far.*

"Miss Reed," the young woman said, extending her hand, her eyes determinedly upon the floor.

I cannot call her by her husband's name! Marianne thought. She disliked the man so much, and yet wanted dearly to like the woman. "Please, call me Marianne! And may I call you Louisa?"

"Of course." She still did not lift her eyes.

"Good! Then, Louisa, would you object to a short walk in the garden? There are benches there, we can sit."

Louisa did not answer, she merely followed her hostess through the house, and into the lovely grounds behind. Marianne led her to the rose garden, where they found a shaded bench, one of Marianne's favourite spots.

"Are you quite settled in your new home?" Marianne asked, watching her new friend closely, assuring herself that Louisa was not tired, or hot.

"Oh, yes. Quite settled."

Marianne wished that she could meet the other woman's eyes. "And the house pleases you?"

"Very much." There was a long silence then, as the hostess tried to figure out how to draw out her guest.

"It must be very difficult to make your home in a strange place, with Captain Weston as your only company," she blurted finally, thoughtlessly, distressed at the long silences in their discourse.

This time, Louisa looked up, her eyes flashing with anger. "Indeed, it is not. One could not hope for better company than Philip!" Her voice caught, and she looked away, but with a show of spirit and emotion, not with shyness and reserve, as before.

Marianne was hurt and ashamed at her own indelicacy. "No, of course not," she replied, her voice low and rich with emotion. "I never meant to imply that he was – I am sure that he is a good husband, and a fine man. I am sorry for what I said. I only meant that it must be difficult to spend all one's time with a single person, and a man at that. After all, a woman needs the company of other women, does she not?"

"I have never found so," Louisa replied. She seemed to have regained a measure of control, but it was though a restraint within her had snapped. She was still reserved, but she no longer appeared to be restraining her voice, her gaze, her movements. Marianne berated herself for her impulsive indiscretion, but noticed with relief that her guest seemed a little more at ease, at last. "I have always been most comfortable in Philip's company," Louisa continued. "One could not wish for a kinder protector."

"Yes," said Marianne, touched by the depth and purity of the other woman's emotion. "I am sure that you are very fortunate to have him as a husband. But I am sure that he is very fortunate also."

"Oh!" Louisa's voice was suddenly tight, almost anguished. "I am not sure that he is so fortunate in his connection with me!"

14

Marianne was surprised, but her companion laughed then, and it was such a sudden, unexpected sound, that she was unsure what to think or how to respond. *There is indeed something to this woman*, she thought. Louisa fell silent, and Marianne turned the conversation to the neighbourhood, and the village. She spoke much, and Louisa listened, saying little herself. After a while, Marianne found that she could find nothing else to say.

The two young women had been sitting quietly on the shaded bench for some time when Mr Reed emerged from the house. Although their silence was not so uncomfortable as the one before, Marianne nonetheless welcomed the interruption.

"Mrs Weston," the elderly man greeted the tiny woman warmly. "I am so glad that you have come to visit us! I am only sorry that I could not come to greet you before."

"Do not be sorry, sir," Louisa replied, rising. "Miss Reed has been a most gracious hostess."

"But you must call her Marianne! All of our friends know my daughter by her Christian name. Indeed, you must call her Marianne!"

"Of course, sir. Marianne–" the woman seemed to be trying the word upon her tongue "–has already bidden me to do so."

"Well then," Mr Reed replied, taking each woman on his arm. "You must come in and take tea with us now. We seldom have guests to tea. We are most often alone at this time of the day, Marianne and I." Both Louisa and Marianne were silent, so Mr Reed continued. "My wife died only five years ago, and our son – that is, Marianne's brother Edmond – has seldom been home since he became an officer in the army several years ago."

Suddenly, Louisa stumbled, an anguished "Ah!" breaking her docile silence. Marianne flew to her side. "Are you all right, Louisa?" she cried. "Have you hurt yourself?"

"No, no, nothing serious," Louisa replied, regaining her composure slightly. "It is only…. I believe that I have turned my ankle. But I am quite all right, I assure you."

Mr Reed summoned a servant, and the three of them helped Mrs Weston to the drawing room, where they were surprised to meet Captain Weston. They learned that a housemaid had been sent to find them in the garden upon his arrival, but had not yet reached them before Louisa's accident.

The Captain rushed to relieve Mr Reed and the coachman of their burden, and helped the frail woman to a sofa. He set her down there, and crouched at her side, examining her ankle with a great care. Marianne was surprised at his tenderness, and the soft, worried expression that cast itself upon his face. Mrs Weston leaned towards him, and murmured something to him, and he replied in an equally intimate tone. Marianne was torn between her determined dislike for the man, and admiration for his kindness and gentleness towards his wife.

"Will she be all right?" Mr Reed asked worriedly.

"Yes, I believe so," Captain Weston replied, standing. "Louisa has not been strong since the birth of her son." Mrs Weston murmured a shocked protest, her face colouring, but her husband took her hand, soothing her.

"I did not know you had children," said Marianne, surprised.

"A son," Louisa said, her eyes cast upon the floor. "His name is James. He is only a year old."

"My eldest child is a son as well," Mr Reed replied jovially. "You are very fortunate, Captain."

Marianne thought she noticed a darkening over Captain Weston's face as he dropped his wife's hand and strode across the room to accept a cup of tea from Marianne. He lingered over it for a moment, swirling it slightly before he brought it back to Mrs Weston. "Very fortunate indeed," he replied, but in a voice so flat and dull that Marianne wondered whether their son were not sickly or infirm. Then she noticed that her friend's hands were shaking as she clasped the hot cup in her palms. Marianne longed to comfort the woman, and wished to know why this comfort was so obviously required. *Perhaps her husband is not very fond of the child*, she mused.

Mr Reed, though a kind and generous man, did not possess his daughter's sensitive and perceptive nature. He did not seem to notice his guests' unease and continued to prattle about his own son as well as theirs. The Westons gave only perfunctory answers, and Marianne felt powerless to assist them. She did not know exactly where the source of their pain lay; how, then, could she divert her father's unintentional barbs from it?

Eventually, however, the conversation turned to more commonplace topics, and Mr Reed and Captain Weston settled into a comfortable discourse. Marianne drew up a chair near by Louisa's seat, and attempted to draw the delicate woman into conversation; Mrs Weston, however, would not be drawn out. The expression of pain and unease had left her face, but her countenance took on no animation as she answered her hostess's questions. She gazed persistently into the fire, and Marianne soon allowed her to lapse into silence, fatigued by the effort of maintaining an almost one-sided conversation.

Finally, Captain Weston announced that it was time to return home. He first assisted his wife into the small, open carriage and returned to take his leave. He spoke for a moment with Mr Reed, then turned to Marianne. She felt the now-familiar sensation of unease uncurl itself in her stomach, like a worm or a butterfly as she faced him. They spoke pleasantries to each other, and she, in her pity and compassion, had almost forgiven his previous rudeness, when he, reaching for his cloak, brushed her shoulder and breast with the back of his hand. She recoiled, unsure whether he had touched her by chance or by design. He straightened, and gazed at Marianne with an expression of both triumph and challenge. Marianne's cheeks grew hot as she gazed back at him in anger and confusion. Her skin where he had touched her burned and tingled, and she caught her breath with difficulty as she challenged his cool, mocking gaze. Then all at once, before she had even fully grasped the brief incident, he was gone, departed to his own home, and Marianne was once again alone with her father, who was speaking to her.

"…fine people, wouldn't you say, my dear?"

"Yes," Marianne managed to stammer, fighting to regain her composure once again. She turned away from him then, and returned to the drawing room, unwilling to allow her father to see her agitation.

Later that evening, Marianne sat alone in her own room, a warm shawl wrapped around her pale shoulders, and gazed out of the darkened window into the cool, clear night. From her bed chamber, she could see the bench where she and Louisa Weston had sat, only a few hours earlier. She had felt, as she sat next to that woman, that Louisa was intentionally maintaining a gulf between them, but that Marianne could bridge it, could secure her trust and her friendship. Now, as she reflected on Captain Weston's inexplicable and inexcusable behaviour, she doubted whether she could ever maintain a friendship with that man's wife. His insinuations the night before had been disgraceful, not only to Marianne, but to Louisa as well. And yet when he had learned of his wife's fall, he had been so tender, so solicitous. Surely, he had some regard, some tenderness for her. Why, then, would he behave in such a manner towards another woman, who was not only a gentlewoman, but also the sister of a friend and fellow officer?

This reflection led Marianne to a frustrating dilemma: should she inform her father of the Captain's impudence? If she did, how would the elderly gentleman react? Certainly, they would stop seeing the Westons. This thought grieved Marianne, as her father would be deprived of his only connection to his only son. However Captain Weston behaved to her, he was certainly kind to Mr Reed. Furthermore, would her father feel obligated to report the Captain's behaviour to other families in the neighbourhood? What, then, would be the effect on Mrs Weston's reputation? She would, of course, be deprived of invitations by the other families. She would be virtually alone, without of the company of her equals. *But would she even care*, Marianne wondered. It seemed as though Louisa were reluctant to seek out any company at all, that it was being forced upon her by her husband. *Nonetheless, I cannot be the one to deprive her of any one who might become her friend!* She could not discuss Captain Weston's behaviour with her father, she decided at last.

This decision, however, did not relieve Marianne's frustrated spirits. Captain Weston's rude, forward behaviour was indeed maddening, and she could not begin to guess at his motives, but it was, to her, almost less shocking than her own reactions to the Captain. In the past, she had often prided herself on her composure and strength of spirit. Even when her mother died, and Marianne felt such grief as she had never felt she would be able to withstand, she had been able to remain strong for her father's sake. Why, then, did she become so tongue-tied and flustered whenever she and the Captain found themselves face-to-face? Why could she not respond to his cruel mischief with the self-possession and indignation that were required to check his behaviour? Marianne grew angry as she thought of her own behaviour to the Captain. Almost involuntarily, she drew her hand up to where his skin had brushed hers. *Why do I allow him to upset me so?* she wondered. *Why can I not treat him as he deserves?*

Marianne was awake long into the night. Her disturbed spirits kept sleep at bay far past the hour at which Marianne was accustomed to giving her body over to rest. When the maid came in the following morning, she found her mistress curled up asleep on the narrow, cushioned window-ledge, with only her shawl to cover her dormant frame.

TWO

Marianne awoke early, her neck stiff, and her head heavy. She stumbled to her bed and fell into an uneasy sleep. For the next few days, a fever confined her to Barronsgate. "That's what comes of sleeping so near the window, Miss," her maid Sarah had said disapprovingly. So, while Sarah served her broth and kept her bedchamber fire stoked so that Marianne felt that she was stifling, it fell upon Mr Reed to visit their neighbours and inquire after Louisa Weston.

"She's quite well, my dear, you needn't worry," he told her one evening, as he sipped his tea. During his daughter's illness, he had taken to dining and taking his tea in her room. She welcomed the company; confinement made her restless, and she longed for variety of any sort.

"Did you see their son, while you were there?" she asked eagerly.

"Yes, indeed. A fine-looking young man, I should say, though I have always found it so hard to judge a baby's looks. I have not a woman's talent for saying whether the child looks more like the mother or more like the father, when they are so young."

"Nor have I," Marianne replied, laughing.

"Even you, my dear," Mr Reed continued, "looked just like every other baby I had ever seen. I'm sorry to say it, but you did. It doesn't matter now, though, since you've grown so lovely. You look so like your mother, only you haven't her fair hair. Edmond does, of course. He didn't look like other babies, for he was always so sickly. He had sores on his face and his neck until he was nearly two years old. Did you know that, Marianne?"

Sipping her tea, Marianne replied that no, she did not.

"It is true, he was a very sickly child. Your mother was so afraid for him. I'm afraid we might have indulged him more than was

21

proper when he was a child. He was rather unmanageable as a boy. I'm not sure if you remember that, Marianne." Here, Marianne made an unintelligible sound into her cup, and her father continued. "'Tis true. I am sad to say it, but 'tis true. Perhaps we were wrong, but I'm afraid we thought he was not long for this world, so we indulged him. It's all turned out for the best, though, I suppose. He's grown up to be a fine young man, and a Captain as well. He has the respect of his men, and he makes such friends as the Westons. So your mother and I worried for nothing. Though I wish she could see how well he's turned out. And you as well, my dear, though there was never a moment's worry about you."

"Father," Marianne said, half-proud, half-ashamed. She reached out her hand to him, and he rose to take it in his own.

"You are so precious to me," he said, his wise, old eyes tearing with pride and love. "What shall I do when you're married and gone away?"

"Who says I shall marry?" she replied, laughing gently. "There is no one that I like half as well as I love you, Father. I am sure that our friends already consider me to be a hopeless spinster. So I shall become an old maid and take care of you forever."

"You shall not," he said, kissing his daughter's forehead. "I won't let you." And then he rose and left Marianne's room, bidding her to rest and get well.

On the third day of her illness, Marianne was well enough to descend to the dining room for dinner. She and her father ate together, sharing a companionable silence for the most part. Afterwards, at Marianne's insistence, they moved to the drawing room, rather than return her to her bedchamber as her father proposed. That morning, he had once again been to the Westons', and Marianne was curious about that family.

"Is Mrs Weston quite recovered from her fall?" she asked as Sarah tucked a shawl about her shoulders.

"Oh, yes, quite. Not even a limp. I believe that she is rather stronger than Captain Weston would have her believe."

"And how is he?" she asked, her voice carefully even and her eyes unflinching.

"Oh, he is well, and the child is well also."

"How is Captain Weston with the child?"

Mr Reed looked up, curious. "What do you mean, my dear?"

"Is he affectionate with the boy? Does he seem to like his son? Does he play with him? What kind of a father is he?" The words tumbled impatiently from her mouth; she was restless and eager, and wanted to find such things out for herself. Despite her affection for her father, his good-natured innocence irritated her somewhat at that moment.

Mr Reed looked up, surprised by his daughter's outburst. He blinked slightly, then continued with his usual kindly implacability. "Oh, to be sure, he is a good father. Though I saw him little with the boy, I am sure of it. And young James is but a baby – rather young for a father to take much notice of him. But he is an attentive husband, and from what I saw, the child lacks nothing. But why such questions, Marianne? Surely you can't doubt that Captain Weston is a good father."

"No, of course not," she replied, smiling and leaning back into her chair. "I am restless here at home. I want news, and if you have none to bring me, I must ask you for some sort of trifling information that will amuse me."

"Oh, my poor Marianne, I forget how tiresome this illness must be for you. If there is anything I can do to make the time pass more quickly, you must tell me."

Marianne laughed tenderly. "You will spoil me, Papa! You mustn't pity me. I will be well tomorrow, you will see."

"I hope that is true," her father replied. "I miss your company on my walks." He paused for a moment, considering. "Shall I send for Charlotte and Antonia Farthington to visit you?"

"No," said Marianne quickly. She did not much like the Farthingtons, and felt that their company would do little good for her health. They were the only gentlewomen of Marianne's age in the neighbourhood, and so, despite Marianne's coolness towards them, the three young ladies were thrown together much. She smiled to soften the harshness of her reply. "No, I would not want to make them ill as well," she added lightly.

"Yes, that is very good of you," Mr Reed replied, picking up a book at his side. Marianne herself let her gaze drift out the windows and onto the lawn. A comfortable silence settled over them.

In the early years of their marriage, Mr and Mrs Reed had grown accustomed to taking daily walks together; these walks had continued until Mrs Reed's illness prevented her from so much exercise. After her death, Marianne, worried that her father's health might also decline, had begun supplying her mother's place, leading her father along the pretty, manicured paths of the Reed estate. And Marianne had come to rely on them as much as her father had, for they provided her with time each day to seek out his counsel, or sound his opinions on books and essays she had read. In short, her father was her dearest friend, and she valued this time with him more than any or all of the items upon Mr Reed's estate, or indeed, more than even the entire estate of Barronsgate itself.

And so, the following day, Marianne was delighted to feel that she was strong enough for a short walk upon the grounds. She allowed Sarah to pile warm shawls upon her shoulders, and indeed, did not complain when her father ordered the gardener to tend a perfectly manicured bit of garden towards the end of their proposed stroll.

As they stepped out onto the lawn, Marianne sniffed the warm August air, and smiled to herself. Her father lagged a bit behind, smiling as he leaned upon his walking stick.

"Father, I should be the one who cannot keep abreast of you," Marianne laughed, taking his free arm. "Have I made you ill?" she asked, suddenly worried.

"I am afraid perhaps a bit feverish," the old man replied, "but I am sure it is nothing that a bit of exercise won't cure."

"Unfair!" Marianne replied, regaining her good humour. "When I am ill, you confine me to bed, and when you are becoming ill, you prescribe exercise for yourself. I say you have gotten the more pleasant cure."

"I am afraid I have, my dear," the elderly gentleman replied placidly. The pair walked on in silence for a moment, until Mr Reed said, "I am sorry, but I'm afraid we really must stop. I believe this fever has caught hold of me more quickly than I anticipated."

"Of course, Father," Marianne said, now genuinely worried. "We'll turn back."

They walked a few steps towards the house, and Mr Reed suddenly stopped, clasped at his daughter's hand, and fell upon the ground. Marianne's shrieks alerted the gardener, who had been hovering near in case the young mistress required assistance in returning to the house.

"Father!" Marianne shrieked, clutching his hand. His breath was laboured, and his eyes were closed. "Father!" He didn't answer her, and his eyelids flickered slightly, but did not open. "Help!" Marianne cried, feeling suddenly desperate and afraid. "Please, please help!"

The gardener rushed to their side and, with Marianne's help, managed to get Mr Reed into the house, and to his bed. The elderly gentleman's face was by now quite grey, and his breath, ragged and uneven. He did not regain consciousness. Marianne, unwilling to leave her father, even for a moment, told Sarah to send for a doctor, and sat anxiously at her father's side, clasping his hand and trying not to cry.

Marianne waited long, impatient hours for the young physician, Mr Christianson, to arrive. There had been some difficulty in locating him, it seemed, as well as some delay in bringing him to Barronsgate, as he had been tending another patient within the village. Marianne refused to leave her father while she waited. Every moment that passed made her feel more and more desperate.

"Go down and see if the doctor is here," she told her maid for what seemed like the thousandth time. The girl obeyed silently, returning a few moments later, only to shake her head, her eyes upon the floor. Marianne fought back tears, pacing the room in quiet, frustrated desperation.

Finally, late that evening, Mr Christianson arrived.

"How long has he been thus?" he asked Marianne as he examined Mr Reed.

"He collapsed suddenly around three this afternoon," she replied, watching anxiously for any sign that her father might be all right. "His condition hasn't changed since then."

"I see," Mr Christianson replied, and finished his examination in

25

silence. He then packed up his instruments, and motioned for Marianne to follow him into the hallway. "I am afraid I see little evidence that he will recover," he said gently, his hand supporting her at the elbow.

"Are you quite sure?" Marianne asked, her eyes cast upon the floor. She did not want him to see her cry.

"Time will tell," he replied, but she knew from his voice that there was little hope. She thanked him, and returned alone to her father's bedside. There, she placed her cheek upon his warm hand and cried bitterly. After her tears had subsided, she remained thus, unwilling to move, lest his condition should change while she was not paying attention. She watched his grey, weathered face, willing him to open his eyes, and to smile at her, telling her that all was well, he was feeling much better now. Marianne watched, her father's hand clasped between her own, but he did not wake. The night wore on, and Marianne remained with her father, sat by him, as his breathing grew more laboured, as his hands lost their warmth, and finally, just before the dawn, Mr Reed slipped quietly into death, leaving his daughter to weep at his side.

Marianne was scarcely aware of the events that surrounded her over the following several days. Her brother was sent for, her brother failed to arrive; her father's friends came and went, and promised help where it was needed; her father was buried, and Marianne returned home to a very empty house.

People of the neighbourhood continued to arrive to pay their respects. Marianne was sensible to their kindness and pity, but craved silence and solitude in order to mourn her father and to weep in private. She moved about the house in a kind of numb grief, that was not soothed or abated by tears or the sympathies of others. Every room seemed to ring with his absence, to crave his quiet kindness as much as his daughter did. And the kind presence of her neighbours only seemed to sharpen his absence. However, several days after Mr Reed's death, Marianne received her first welcome visitor. She had been sitting near the fire, her hair pulled back into a slightly dishevelled knot, her gown, newly dyed black, bunching about her legs. The kindly maid Sarah, who had been presiding over her grief-

stricken mistress, whispered that Mrs Weston had arrived to see her.
"Oh," Marianne replied, as though she had just been awoken
from a deep slumber. She rose, and straightened her gown, preparing
to meet her visitor.

Mrs Weston entered soundlessly, and stood for a long moment,
gazing at Marianne, as though attempting to solve a riddle. Then
with sudden decidedness, she crossed the room, and embraced
Marianne wordlessly. Marianne collapsed against the young woman,
gratefully accepting her kindness, and sobbed against her shoulder.
They stood thus for a long while, not speaking, Mrs Weston stroking
Marianne's back as she cried. Finally Marianne stood, her tears
spent, and gazed at her friend, touched and surprised to discover that
Louisa was crying too.

"You are so kind to come," Marianne said, wiping her cheeks
with her handkerchief, and leading Louisa to the chair where her
father had been accustomed to sit. Marianne herself had been unable
to approach it, but now she welcomed the comfort that she sought
from its inhabitant, as she had so many times in the past.

"Is there anything I can do for you, Marianne? Any small thing
that I can bring you, that will give you some comfort?"

"Thank you, you have done that already," she replied, sinking
into her own chair. "Now, if you please, distract me with some small
story about your own family. How is the little one?"

Louisa blushed in reply. "Oh, he is well – very well. He seems to
be growing every minute. I sometimes feel that I shall leave him in
the care of the nurse one morning, and return that afternoon to find
that he is a grown man, with a wife and children of his own!"

"Oh, surely it is not so!" Marianne laughed. "Does he walk yet?"

"A little. He holds my hands and stumbles along. He will be a
very strong man one day, I believe."

"Like his father."

Louisa's smile faded, and she gazed into the fire. "Yes.... I
believe he will be very much like his father. I worry he will be too
much so." And she turned back to her companion, and smiled once
again, but there was a strange sadness in her eyes.

"Oh, but young men are often like their mothers in temper and
disposition. I am sure of it. My own brother is very high-spirited, as

was my mother. Louisa, have you ever met Edmond?"

"Yes – that is, I knew him slightly in Somersetshire."

"Oh, were you Somersetshire?"

"Yes, I was visiting with my – my family when your brother was there. I know him only slightly."

"That is probably best," Marianne replied wryly. "Edmond is best known in small quantities. He – has a kind heart, but I'm afraid he can be somewhat of a rake." Marianne perceived then that Louisa's face had reddened, and she wondered whether their acquaintance had not occurred before the Westons were married. Tactfully, she changed the subject, spoke of more trivial things, until her friend had recovered her composure. Then they spoke for some time longer, before Louisa regretfully said that she must return home.

"I hate to leave little James alone for long," she confessed. "And I'm afraid that I miss him more than he does me."

"Oh, then bring him along when you visit me next," Marianne exclaimed, rising. She was ashamed that she could not extend the invitation to Captain Weston with the same sincerity. "I should very much like to meet him."

"I shall," Louisa promised, embracing her friend one last time. "When might I return to pay you another visit?"

"Oh, soon, very soon!"

"All right, I shall see you soon then," Louisa replied, and embraced her friend once again before departing.

And Louisa was gone once again, leaving Marianne on her own. She sat by the fire, and her grief for her father soon led her to miss both of her parents, so that Sarah, coming in a quarter of an hour later, found her crying once again. But here tears were not the same empty, disconsolate sobs that Sarah had seen racking her mistress' body since Mr Reed's death, and the little maid felt suddenly relieved of her fears for Marianne. With tears in her own eyes, she shut the door quietly, leaving Miss Reed to her sorrow and her relief.

The following day, Louisa arrived as she had promised, and brought her young son with her as well. Marianne was delighted with the bright, lively child, and would not allow her guests to leave before she had secured from then a promise that they would return on the next day as well. Consequently, on that morning, she was not surprised to hear a carriage pull up before noon. However, it was not Mrs Weston who was admitted into the drawing room at Barronsgate, but Captain Weston.

"Miss Reed," he said, bowing. "Allow me to express my condolences."

"Thank you," she replied, offering him a seat. Her sorrow and exhaustion almost prevented her from experiencing that now-familiar twinge in her stomach that occurred every time they met.

He sat, and for a moment, seemed at a loss for words. "I wanted to inquire," he said finally, "what your plans are now."

"My plans?" *What is he trying to ask*, she wondered.

"Where do you intend to live?"

Marianne was taken aback by the strange question. "Why, here," she replied frankly. "My brother Edmond is heir, but I cannot imagine that he would wish me to leave. And my father has provided me with a sufficient income. I see no reason to leave."

"I see." And Captain Weston leaned back, surveying her with an expression that frightened Marianne.

"May I ask, Captain, why you ask these questions?" *What business of yours is it where I choose to live?*

"I'm afraid, Miss Reed, that I have some news that must be.... Well, it must be unwelcome." It occurred to Marianne that he had the air of one who very much wanted to be enjoying himself, but was instead anguished and distraught.

"Does this news concern by brother?"

"I'm afraid that it does. You see, your brother has managed to accumulate some debts."

"Debts, Captain?"

"Yes, debts. Rather considerable debts, in fact. In Edinburgh, in Brighton, London, even a few abroad."

"And you fear that these debts will threaten his estate?" Marianne was trying desperately to divine Captain Weston's role in this affair. Why was he telling her of Edmond's debts?

"I'm afraid it already has. You see, I have gone to some trouble to relieve your brother of these debts. This has been going on for some time, and Edmond has written me a promissory note that I'm afraid he cannot hope to fulfil unless he sells Barronsgate."

"Sells Barronsgate?" Marianne was feeling weak and dizzy. She felt the blood drain from her face. "But surely his debts–"

"Aren't equal to the value of Barronsgate? You are right; however, I am acquainted with your brother's income – both as a Captain, and that from his tenants here at Barronsgate. And he cannot possibly hope to accumulate a sufficient sum from that income to repay – what he now owes me. I'm afraid that, until he decides to sell his estate, Barronsgate is, for all purposes, my own."

"I see," Marianne replied quietly. She surveyed Captain Weston's face. It was cool and implacable, but she believed that she witnessed there equal parts of triumph and pity. It seemed to her that he was gazing upon the misfortune of some inferior creature, undeserving of his respect or of happiness of any kind. Her shock and sorrow dissipated, and anger took its place. *What kind of man can be so self-satisfied in the presence of the misery of others?* she wondered. *And who is he that he thinks I want or need his pity?*

"I'm terribly sorry," he said, his voice dry and cool.

"Don't," Marianne snapped, rising. "Don't attempt to ply me with your insincere condolences. I want none of them. I assure you, sir, I shall discuss this with my brother. We will find another solution. I do not believe that you are right in your assessment of what must be done."

Captain Weston rose also, and pulled a letter out of his pocket. "I believe that this must convince you," said he, handing it to her.

Marianne took it from him, fighting back tears of rage and humiliation. She began to read, and sank heavily back upon her chair, a feeling of despair washing over her. The letter was from Edmond – she recognised his handwriting – and was addressed to Captain Weston. In it were a vague account of the debts he had accumulated, though without any way of fixing their exact amount. In it also, Edmond had acknowledged that he now owed this money to Weston. He had pledged the income from Barronsgate upon his father's death to Weston, as repayment, and he had even promised to sell Barronsgate if Weston found the income to be unsatisfactory. In essence, he had given his home – his family's home, Marianne's own home – to this man until all that he owed him was repaid!

For a long while, Marianne could not say anything at all. Captain Weston remained standing as before, waiting for her to speak, or, she supposed, to return the letter that promised him a small fortune. She had an urge to throw it into the fire; instead, she folded it carefully, and released it into his outstretched hand. She dared not look at his beguiling grey eyes now, for fear of what she might find there. Instead, she gazed numbly into the fire. "Go, Captain," she said at least. "Please go. We will discuss this tomorrow." She did not look up, but traced instead his exit by the sound of his boots to the front entrance and out the door. Then she closed her eyes, and leaned her head upon the chair, unable to rage or weep. She knew this house so well, that she knew by the slightest sound where each person was within its walls. It was almost a part of her. She could move from room to room blindfolded, never once stumbling upon an article of furniture, or bumping her delicate nose upon a wall or a doorway. How could she leave it, release it into this stranger's custody? How could she imagine a life for herself outside of its kind, comforting, familiar walls? Without Barronsgate, Marianne would feel incomplete, lost, amputated.

Soon, she began to think of her brother, or his recklessness and irresponsibility and utter selfishness. *How could he possibly amass such debts?* she wondered hopelessly. He was not a young man of inadequate means; besides his income from the militia, he had no small amount of wealth as only son and heir of Barronsgate. All at once, rage and anguish built up within her, and burst forth in a long, tortured cry that brought the kindly Sarah running to her mistress. But when she arrived, Marianne was already sobbing quietly into her handkerchief, so that all Sarah could do was to stroke her hair and utter meaningless words of comfort, unheard by the young woman in her grief and her helplessness.

THREE

Marianne slept little that night, though the kindly Sarah brought her young mistress every comfort she could think of. "My mother served your mother, Miss," she said gently, "when you and I were but young girls. I knew her as well as anyone outside your family could. And I know that Mrs Reed would want you to be strong. All will be well. You will see." But Marianne would only stare mutely, not drinking the warm wine that Sarah handed her, not eating the sweetmeats that she put before her. Finally, Sarah herself retired to bed, leaving Marianne alone with her grief and her frustration. Marianne had ceased to wonder how her brother could have accumulated such a debt, ceased to wonder how he could simply hand over their family home to a man with whom only he himself had an acquaintance, had even ceased to be angry with him. *What's the use?* she wondered. How could she be angry with someone whose actions were so very irresponsible in their nature that they could have no logical explanation? It was only near the dawn that it finally occurred to Marianne to become apprehensive about her own situation. After all, she had no home, no one to take her in, and only a small income of her own to live on. A pit of despair formed itself in her stomach. She rose, agitated, and dressed, though the sun had not yet risen, and she had not yet slept. She pulled her hair back severely, the contents of Edmond's letter to Captain Weston repeating themselves in her mind.

I appreciate your assistance with the small affair of my debts ... my own income, as well as that from Barronsgate is yours ... please consider my home your own ... I will sell it if necessary....

Marianne's jaw tightened at her brother's cruel, callous thoughtlessness. How could he have pledged their family home to a man who was a stranger to them all? And to have done it while her father was still alive! Her only comfort was that Mr Reed had died knowing nothing of his son's selfishness and irresponsible acts. And still, Marianne longed for his guidance and his gentle wisdom, as she prepared herself for the interview that she must endure with Captain Weston, who was now, she recognised, master of her own fate.

She breakfasted alone as soon as the sun broke upon the house, and set off by horse towards Trent Cottage. It was a clear, bright morning, and at any other time, Marianne would have taken pleasure in the ride, might perhaps have stopped to admire the view by the roadside, or sample the blackberries from the hedge. Today, however, she rode on grimly and without joy. She had determined that Weston would not dominate this interview as he had the day before; she must meet him at his home, rather than allowing him to catch her at a disadvantage once again. She kept her horse in a brisk trot, and firmly resisted the impulse to turn it back towards Barronsgate, towards all that had always been familiar and safe and comforting to her.

She arrived at the Cottage just as the Westons had finished their own breakfast. She refused to look at Louisa or her young son, lest the sight of her friend should cause her to lose her firm resolve. Instead, she requested a private meeting with the Captain in his study.

"Of course," he replied, bowing coolly: the model of impersonal good manners. He led her into his study, invited her to sit, then sat down himself, waiting calmly for her to begin. His own composure shook Marianne's, as she fought to retain control of her emotions. His grey eyes surveyed her with interest, it seemed to her, but without curiosity. She drew herself up to meet them.

"Captain Weston," she began, hoping that her voice did not sound as shrill to his ears as it did to her own. "I have considered the unfortunate situation that we now find ourselves in, due to my brother's ... regrettable financial tendencies. Of course, you must be compensated without delay for the money you put forth on his behalf. As you are well aware, my father's income is now Edmond's." Here, her throat tightened, and her eyes burned, but she forced herself to continue, fighting back the softened emotions that threatened to overtake her. She hurried her speech, unwilling to break down before she had said what she needed to say. "I also understand that your residence at Trent Cottage must come at a considerable expense to you. I would like to propose that, in order to reduce my family's debt to you as expediently as possible, you and your family take residence at Barronsgate."

The Captain's eyes flickered with evident, though contained surprise, and Marianne's chest tightened. He was silent, and Marianne felt as though she was being pulled into his clear, penetrating gaze. She fought the urge to blush or fidget, meeting his eyes with what she hoped was an equal cool composure on her own part. Finally, he spoke, leaning forward slightly as he did so. His voice was rich and low.

"That is a very interesting proposition, Miss Reed," he said at last. "And where do you propose to take up residence, yourself, during this time?" She believed that a note of dry amusement had found its way into his words.

"At Barronsgate, Captain," she replied sharply. "It is no small home. I believe that you will find there is room for us all."

"And you will remain there, unescorted, unprotected?"

Marianne felt her cheeks grow hot, she drew herself up, meeting his gaze. "I do not know why I would need protection in my own home," she replied. "Especially in the presence of such *friends of my family*," the words burned upon her tongue, envenomed and ironic, "as yourself and Mrs Weston."

The Captain laughed then, his voice reverberating throughout the otherwise silent room. "Indeed, Miss Reed," he said, "and Heaven help anyone who might ever presume to put you in need of any protection. I believe that you yourself would make short work of any such person."

"You are quite right, I would. And you must remember that I am not entirely without friends, sir." She clenched her jaw and met his eyes unflinchingly.

Suddenly, Captain Weston's smile faded, he looked at her so intently then that she was unable to hold his gaze; she turned instead to the window, her back to him.

"Not entirely," she heard him say, though his voice was so low he seemed to be speaking for himself alone. "But almost." He made

35

no further move to speak to her, and she was forced to break the silence and stillness in the room. She turned, but kept her gaze upon the floor, instead of on him.

"So it is settled then. You and your family will move into Barronsgate as soon as it is convenient for you." She turned then, striding determinedly from the room, refusing to allow herself to lose any of the advantage that she still might have. She felt confused, however, unsure whether the interview had belonged to him or to her. Nonetheless, she left the house with what she knew was a cool dignity, mounted her horse, rode out of the view of the Cottage, and promptly burst into tears.

She allowed herself to sob freely as her horse plodded along the secluded lane, but as her own home came into sight, she forced herself to stop crying. She wiped her face ruthlessly of its tears, and straightened herself in the saddle. Coaxing the horse into a trot, she rode towards the stables, then pulled up in front of a young groom and allowed him to help her dismount. She strode purposefully into the house, took off her cloak, and fought the feeling of dismay and helplessness that threatened to overcome her. She wanted to collapse, to demand that someone care for her; instead, she opened the doors to her father's library, and walked slowly in. She sat down at his desk, and searched for a fresh sheet of paper, tears filling her eyes. She gritted her teeth and fought them back. *Enough crying*, she scolded herself. *It won't do – I will have to learn to be much stronger now.* Her cheeks dry and her eyes burning, she began her letter.

Dear Edmond, she wrote. She was unable to continue. *How could you do this?* she wanted to write, *How could you be so selfish?* or *What am I to do to fix what you have broken?* Instead, she wrote nothing. He could not possibly care what happened to her or to their home, if he could so carelessly promise Barronsgate to a man who was a stranger to everyone but him. She sat, staring at the blank page, then finally she gave up, tearing the page to pieces, and tossing it into the fire. This time, the tears that streamed down her face were tears of rage. She pushed at them with her fingers, angry and ashamed with herself. She stood, and a fuzzy blackness encroached upon her vision, then her thoughts. She staggered forward, unable to regain her clarity. Then she was falling, spinning, unable to grasp anything as she tumbled. She welcomed the warm oblivion that enveloped her.

When Marianne awoke, she became aware of a strong, cool hand pressing itself upon her cheek. She sighed, feeling warm and safe. She could hear a woman's voice at the edge of her thoughts, and realised it was Sarah's. There was a man's voice too, familiar, yet without a name in Marianne's mind. She blinked, trying to focus on the source of these sounds. Dark, wavy hair became clear in her gaze, then a warm, sun-darkened complexion, and finally, clear grey eyes. Marianne blinked, trying to understand where she was, and how she had gotten there.

"Oh Miss Marianne!" Sarah's tearful voice pulled her attention away. "You are awake! I am so glad you're all right! Thank heavens for Captain Weston!"

"Captain Weston!" Marianne's mouth felt thick, cottony. She pulled away from the Captain, who, she was now aware, was supporting her at the waist. Her legs, however, were still weak and unsteady, ands she found that she had to submit to his assistance in finding a chair.

"I left Trent Cottage soon after you did," he said. There was a warmth in his voice that she had never heard before. "When I arrived here, Sarah directed me to your father's study. As I entered, you were just rising from the desk. I don't believe you heard me announce myself. You seemed unsteady, so I reached out my hand to assist you. Then suddenly, you fell. Fortunately, I was there to catch you, or you might have been hurt."

"I did not even know you were there," she replied in dismay. She allowed Sarah to remove her slippers and cover her feet with a warm shawl.

"It's lucky he was, Miss," Sarah said, her own face pale and worried. Marianne squeezed her hand gratefully.

"Why did you come, Captain?" Marianne asked, turning her attention back to him. He had retreated to a corner of the study, was in fact leaning upon the same desk where she herself had been sitting.

He looked away at this question, looking sheepish, almost

ashamed. "Such business can wait until you are feeling better, Miss Reed," he murmured, not looking at her.

"Nonsense," she said, drawing herself up. Her head, however, had begun to hurt in a thick, throbbing manner, so she refrained from standing. "What business caused you to follow me back to my home?"

"I will return tomorrow, we can converse then." And he began to stride towards the door.

"Captain! You will do me the courtesy of explaining your visit." She was aware that her voice had achieved the shrill tone that often crept into her speech when she got annoyed. He did not answer, and Marianne called out to him again. "Do you hear me, sir? I demand that you explain yourself! Stop at once!"

The Captain stopped short, his shoulders tense. He spun abruptly, his cheeks coloured and his eyes flashing. "Since you demand to know, Miss," he said, his voice cold and sharp, "I will not disappoint you. Louisa, James and I will begin our residence here within the week." He started to leave, but turned to her once more before his departure. "James will require a nursery, with an adjoining room for his nurse. And Louisa sleeps ill – she will need a chamber of her own." With that, he spun on his heel and strode out of the room. Marianne heard the front door close, and sat, breathless with shock.

"Their residence!" Sarah exclaimed. "Whatever does he mean, Miss?"

But Marianne was unable to reply. She sat silently, attempting to comprehend what she had just heard. In less than seven days, she must share her home with that man and his family. Tears threatened to spill from her eyes, but she refused herself this weakness. At long last, she was able to respond to Sarah's anxious inquiries.

"Prepare yourselves," she said to Sarah, but loudly enough that any of the other servants in earshot might understand her. "We are to have guests."

Suddenly faced with the necessity of informing the household servants of the imminent change of situation within Barronsgate, but unwilling to reveal the extent of the family's troubles, Marianne felt a strong desire to remove herself from the constant, subtle bustle of the house. She decided to ride out upon its grounds, where she was unlikely to encounter grooms or gardeners, cooks or maids.

"If you must go out, Miss," Sarah pleaded following Marianne out towards the stables, "only allow Paul or another of the grooms to ride out with you."

"No, Sarah," Marianne replied, fastening on her bonnet. "I'll ride alone today."

"But you are unwell. Only this morning, the Captain–"

"Enough, Sarah!" she snapped, annoyed at the young servant's intrusion. "I'm not in the habit of fainting, and it is not an experience that I intend to repeat. I said I will ride out alone, and I will ride out alone!" Without another word, she strode away, accepting the reins wordlessly from the abashed young groom Paul, who had overheard the exchange. She rode out north of the house, to a gently wooded area where, she remembered, her father and Edmond had spent many days hunting, so long ago now. There, she slowed her mount to a walk, and allowed herself to allow the gentle beauty of her surroundings. It was so quiet, so peaceful that she could almost forget the great difficulties she had to face.

"But I cannot forget my duties," she said out loud. "For there is no one else to tend to them." Strangely, the thought did not frighten her; instead, she drew herself up, feeling like a medieval knight about to face a great challenger. *I am alone*, she realised, *but I am not helpless*. She took the reins firmly in her hands and coaxed her horse into a brisk trot towards the house. Instead of returning immediately, however, she allowed herself the pleasure of an invigorating ride upon the grounds. She arrived at last at the house, flushed and tired, but not humbled or broken. She handed the reins to young Paul, and strode into the house, calling for Sarah.

"Assemble the servants after dinner," she said, unpinning her bonnet. "I must speak to you all."

"Yes, Miss," Sarah replied, curtseying. Marianne saw by her eyes that she had been crying; her heart softened, but she did not repent her earlier harshness. *They must learn to respect me*, she thought to herself. *Until the debt is discharged or Edmond returns, I am mistress here.* The thought did not displease her, though it came with a pang of loneliness for her father.

Marianne ate alone in the dining room, taking care not to appear hurried or eager. Finally, she laid down her fork and her napkin and rose slowly, smoothing her dress and drawing a deep breath. Maintaining what she hoped was a silent dignity, she strode into the front hall, where the servants were nervously grouped, awaiting her announcement. She fought back the waves of nervousness that threatened her, and strode out in front of them. She blinked as she glanced across their expectant faces, then began.

"As you must all know already," she said, "we are soon to have guests. My brother's friends the Westons will be arriving to stay with us by the end of the week. The length of their stay is yet undetermined. I would like you to prepare Edmond's chamber for Captain Weston, and the nursery for young James. I know that it has suffered under its long disuse, but I have faith that you will render it serviceable. As for Mrs Weston, please prepare my mother's chamber for her." Marianne's throat tightened, but she breathed deeply and forced herself to continue. "For the meantime, please leave my father's chamber as it is." With that, Marianne strolled regally to her own chamber, where she relished in the solitude and the comfort. She sat at the window, staring over the grounds, and hoped that she could find the strength from within herself that she had attempted to present to the servants that day. *I do my best to act in a manner that would make you proud, Papa*, she thought, valiantly fighting back the tears that were already streaming down her cheeks.

In due course, the end of the week arrived at Barronsgate, and so did the Westons. Marianne did her best to act the part of the gracious hostess, refusing to Captain Weston the role of an indulgent landlord for allowing her to stay.

"This will be your room," she said, opening the door for Louisa.

"It's quite lovely," Mrs Weston replied, walking to the window and surveying the gardens beyond. "Why do you not sleep here?"

"This room was my mother's," Marianne replied quietly, joining her friend at the window.

"Oh!" Louisa's voice was shocked. She turned to Marianne, her eyes wide and childlike in her alarm. "Then I must not stay here!"

"No, indeed," Marianne replied warmly, sincerely, taking her friend's hand. "You must. It would give me pleasure to know that this room is so well-used."

"Are you quite sure, Marianne?" Louisa asked hesitantly, like a young girl seeking her parents' approval.

"Quite." In fact, Marianne had considered the guest rooms in the far wing of Barronsgate for the Westons. Those rooms were so seldom used, however, that Marianne felt wrong consigning Louisa and her son to their distant draughtiness. And it pleased her, she realised, to have Louisa, whom Marianne had come to care very deeply for, in her mother's room. Mrs Weston would be a comforting presence for her friend.

Marianne smiled suddenly. "And now let us go and see how young James likes his own room!" As they left, she closed the door behind them, gently and without regret.

Through careful management, Marianne managed to spend much of the following few days with Mrs Weston and James, and avoided the Captain almost altogether. She was civil to him when they dined together at breakfast and at tea; her other meals, Marianne took alone in her room or her father's study, which the Westons had wisely chosen to leave to Marianne's almost exclusive use. The other rooms of the stately house, however, were soon filled with sights, sounds and smells that were rather more Weston than Reed. Marianne fought the urge to rail at these subtle intrusions, reminding herself that it was she who had invited them into her home, and that, indeed, it was now as much theirs as it was hers. Still, she could not help but wonder what reasons the Captain had given his wife for their move; Marianne herself was unable to breach the subject with Louisa. She felt that, should they discuss the Reeds' difficulties, she must necessarily lose her only ally, her only friend. So instead, they spoke of other things: of the warm, moist weather, of the books from Mr Reed's library that Marianne lent to Louisa, and often, of little James.

The youngest Weston was a lusty young chap, whose vivid, energetic temperament often pleased Marianne more than it did his own mother. Marianne quickly grew to love James, and began to feel that he had always been a part of her own family, that he, like her, was a member of the household, and that he too must learn to endure the intrusion of his own parents. He was energetic and inquisitive, and like his mother, he was sweet-tempered and affectionate, but he had none of the pensive sullenness that Marianne so often encountered in the Captain. Indeed, it was probably because he was so little like his father that Marianne loved him so quickly and so dearly.

As summer turned to fall, Marianne spent her days in as pleasant company as she could desire, without wishing for her own father to be restored to her (which she nonetheless did wish, as she sat in his study in quiet solitude). Her evenings, she spent alone, remembering and regretting her father, all the while refusing to resort to despair and self-pity. And for her own part, she was grateful that respect for her father prevented Captain Weston from renewing his insinuations to her. Indeed, he seemed to pay as little attention to her as he did Mrs Frawley the housekeeper, or Paul the groom or Sarah the maid. And though Marianne had suspected him to be a man of vice, there was no evidence about him of gambling or of drink or of whores. And while he was not overly attentive to Louisa and James, he was nonetheless unfailingly courteous to them, and sensitive to their needs and their happiness. In short, Marianne became inclined to judge him somewhat less harshly than she had before.

One evening, after a late stroll about the grounds with Louisa, who was daily becoming more open and candid with her friend and hostess, Marianne stopped in the drawing room for a moment's rest before retiring for the night. Sarah, whose attentions to her mistress had never faltered since Mr Reed's death, brought Marianne some warm milk to sip by the fire. "So you don't take cold again, Miss," the kind young servant said, before she herself retired for the night. Marianne was enjoying the warmth of the fire and of the honey-sweetened beverage in solitude as Captain Weston entered.

"Am I disturbing you, Miss Reed?" he asked. Without waiting for her answer, he sat down opposite her.

"Not at all," she replied, wishing he would leave her to her solitude.

"I am glad that you and Louisa have become such dear friends," he said with a slight smile upon his full lips.

"I have nothing but the greatest affection for your wife and son."

Why won't he leave?

"It is well that we should all be close friends, since we are to share a home for some time." He leaned back in his chair, and the firelight played across his handsome, angular features.

Marianne felt her cheeks grow hot. "Indeed!"

"I trust that it is not too unpleasant, sharing your home." The Captain dropped his tone to a warm, conspiratory level. His magnetic grey eyes invited her to ... *to what?* she wondered. And yet she did not fight their appeal.

"No, not unpleasant," she replied, feeling unaccountably troubled. He was leaning close to her, and she could see the beginnings of lines that had formed themselves around his cool, beguiling eyes. His eyes seemed older than the rest of his face, or his proud, strong bearing. She could not help but wonder what cares had caused those lines to appear.

The Captain was silent for some time, but unlike Marianne, he seemed perfectly at his ease. He gazed into the fire, his long, graceful limbs sprawled in an almost regal pose, lit to advantage in the flickering firelight. Marianne could not help but admire his masculine grace, his strong features, his gentle, curving, almost effeminate mouth. She wanted to say something, to break his spell of composure, but even more, she wanted it to endure, to be able to survey him, to watch the play of the firelight in his dark hair. All at once, she became aware that as she watched him, he was watching her. Her breath caught, and his lips curled slightly.

"You are lovely in the firelight, Marianne," he said softly. Her lips parted, but she found herself unable to respond. He leaned forward, and she felt nervousness, anticipation almost; still, she was unable to move, unable to speak. He stood, and took her hand in his. It was warm and strong, and it did not occur to her to pull her own hand from his grasp. She did not wonder what would now happen, she merely waited. They remained thus for perhaps a small eternity, and she found that she too had risen, though she did not remember doing so. The curving smile on his lips fascinated, fixated her.

"You seem tired, Miss Reed," he said at last, his tone cool and level once more. Marianne blinked, attempting to focus.

"Yes," she replied. "Yes, I am."

"Perhaps you should retire. You and Louisa have taken much exercise today."

"Yes," she said again, and allowed him to lead her to the doorway. She walked into the hall and mounted the stairs towards her own room, still unable to decipher to herself what had just occurred. She paused upon the stairs and turned. The Captain remained in the doorway of the drawing room, studying her with his cool, impenetrable eyes. A gentle smile once again curved his lips, but now his countenance seemed cool, controlled, even slightly mocking. She gazed at him for a moment, as one does when, just awakened, one is trying to determine what strange place it is that they have slept in. Then she turned again, climbed the last few stairs, and walked slowly to her bedroom, closing the door softly behind her.

FOUR

Marianne Reed was lively and intelligent; her parents had provided the best tutors for their children. Her acquaintance with the Westons, however, was quickly teaching her the painful lesson of her own naïveté, the product of her sheltered, secluded life. Barronsgate was an out-of-the-way estate, and the neighbourhood had offered her few opportunities to interact with potential suitors. Mrs Reed had died when Marianne was yet too young to be much in society, and since then, Mr Reed had shown little inclination to experience the gay scenes of London or Brighton, and had never been able to propose pleasant trips abroad without the company of his wife. And their neighbours consisted mainly of conservative and retiring gentlefolk of Mr Reed's own age, and of daughters as inexperienced as Miss Marianne Reed herself. Young men were somewhat of a rarity in that neighbourhood. Marianne had always felt sure of herself. She felt a deep sense of right and wrong, but now, in the absence of her father and in the presence of her unlikely guardians Mr and Mrs Weston, she was discovering how untested her moral education had been. She began to realise that she was at once clever and naïve, perceptive and innocent. She felt suddenly unbalanced, blinded and lost, where she had once believed herself to be unfailingly sure, secure in her own rightness. For the first time in her life, she was experiencing doubt in a serious way. Consequently, though she felt an acute unease about her evening encounter with Captain Weston, and had already discovered the potential for a certain baseness and forwardness in his nature, she was unable to determine what exactly in their encounter caused her so much disquiet. *Perhaps he was acting with the kindness that any man might show to the friend of his wife*, she thought doubtfully; despite her lingering dislike for the Captain, she was loath to attribute to him the worst motives in the affair. Furthermore, she was left entirely without counsel in the matter, for as Louisa was her only confidante, who would hear such suspicions about Captain Weston?

The morning after her encounter in the drawing room with Captain Weston, Marianne rose late, and breakfasted in her own room. She felt uninclined to join the rest of the household; instead, she sat in her window-seat, still in her dressing gown, her hair tumbling and tangled on her shoulders, reading a favourite volume of poetry. She soon found, however, that her mind was not on her book. Her gaze fell upon the garden and the uncommonly warm September day outside. Some time after noon, Louisa and her son strolled out onto the lawn to sit and play together. Marianne's attention was caught by the charming family scene. Louisa was making monkeyish faces at little James, who was laughing with delight. Marianne soon found that she, too, was laughing at the antics of her friend. *Sometimes she is so like a child herself!* she reflected. After some time, Captain Weston joined his family on the lawn. Louisa curbed her behaviour, and Marianne's smile faded. The Captain seated himself on the lawn next to his wife, yet without touching her. He played with James, allowed him to tug at his hair and his clothes, and smiled at the bright, inquisitive young boy. He talked to Louisa, who replied with easy smiles and gentle laughter, and Marianne felt an inexplicable pang in the pit of her stomach. *Does he take her hand and speak to her as he did to me?* she wondered painfully.

The thought came to her as a great surprise. She rose and shook herself. "Well, of course he might," she said aloud. "They're married! Surely if he would share such confidential moments with me, he and Louisa must share such times between themselves!" But the thought made her agitated, unhappy even, and she turned to the window once again.

She gazed upon the couple on the lawn below, and without warning, Captain Weston shifted his gaze upon her window. For a moment, Marianne felt herself incapable of moving. Then the Captain cast upon her a slow, lazy smile, a confidential smile, and Marianne broke away from the window.

"Enough!" she said, trying to ignore her own sudden agitation. "I must spend my day in more useful pursuits than gazing out upon the lawn!" She tied back her hair impatiently, dressed in her riding gear and descended down the back stairs, walking briskly in the direction of the stables.

She strolled leisurely from the house, enjoying the warm, quiet morning. The crunch of gravel behind her made her spin about. She was expecting a groom or a gardener; instead, she found herself face-to-face with Captain Weston!

"Oh!" she said, without thinking. "I thought you were out on the lawn!"

"Indeed I was," he replied, smiling slowly, lazily. "I thought I would take a ride. I see I am not alone in that desire."

"Yes," Marianne said, looking at her riding clothes. "In which direction were you planning to ride?" *So that I might take the opposite direction.*

"Well, since we are of the same mind, might we not ride together?"

"Of course. Please get my horse then." Marianne tugged at her gloves to hide her annoyance.

Weston stood still for a moment, looking at her. Then he bowed slightly, and moved towards the stable. As he passed her, however, he spun, clutching her arm. He leaned towards her, his breath upon her hair. "I am not your servant," he whispered coolly. "I won't take orders from you, Miss Reed. It might even be debated which one of us two is the guest in this house. Fetch your own horse." With that, he strode into the stable, emerging a few moments later with his own horse. "Hurry up then," he said, mounting. "Let us ride before the sun sets."

Marianne stood speechlessly as hot blood rushed to her face. Her furious glare seemed to have no effect upon Weston – he surveyed her calmly, pleasantly even from his seat in the saddle. Wordlessly, she spun upon her heel and stalked into the house, slamming the door behind her. She watched through the window, waiting for him to leave. She saw, or thought she saw the little smile that tugged at the edge of his lips as he watched the door a moment, as though waiting for her to emerge once again. Finally, coolly, he turned his horse away and rode nonchalantly down the lane.

After she had watched the Captain gallop off alone, when she was sure he was out of sight, Marianne re-emerged, had the groom prepare her horse and trotted alone from the house. *I will not make my plans according to the Captain's conduct*, she thought angrily. She turned her horse towards Trent Cottage, which had a pretty lane of its own. She had seen the Captain head in the opposite direction, so she did not think that she would encounter him. She rode leisurely, enjoying the warm sun, admiring the lovely, familiar countryside, and at last turned her horse homeward, pleased that she had managed to avoid Weston. As she approached Barronsgate, however, he came suddenly upon her, and when he saw Marianne, he reined in his horse to wait for her.

"I hope you have had a good ride, Miss Reed," he said.

"Very," she replied coolly, trotting past him. He caught up, and rode beside her in silence for a short time. Finally, in frustration, Marianne slowed her horse to a walk. The Captain did the same.

"Is there something you would like to discuss with me, Captain?" she asked peevishly.

"Not at all. And surely by now you may call me Philip and I shall call you Marianne."

She flushed with anger. "I have asked you once before not to use my Christian name, *Captain* Weston!"

"Oh? And yet you did not protest last evening!"

Marianne was confused. She did not remember him using her name ... and yet so much of the evening was hazy to her. She tossed her head slightly and replied, "I am telling you now. I wish you to address me more civilly–"

"Accuse me of anything but incivility," the Captain laughed. "You and Louisa address each other by your Christian names, do you not? Indeed, you are so much like sisters by now that I wish you to take a more sisterly affection to me. We live in the same house, as do brother and sister, cannot we be more so ourselves?"

"I wish you to be anything but my brother," Marianne replied hotly.

The Captain laughed a low, suggestive laugh. "Why, then so do I, my dear Marianne. It's settled. I will be *anything but* your brother!"

48

Marianne reined up her horse suddenly and dismounted, thrusting the reins in the Captain's direction. "Return my horse to the stables. I have no wish to ride any further with you!" She spun around, stalking angrily towards the house, but before she had taken two steps, the Captain was down upon the ground beside her, grasping her arms roughly. Marianne cried out in pain and surprise.

"That is the second time today you have attempted to order me about, Miss Reed," he said. His face was very close to hers, his grey eyes spitting fire, his breath warm on her cheek. She tried to twist away, but he held her tight. "I am not your servant, I will not take orders from you! Remember that in the future." Then suddenly, brutally, he released her, and she stumbled backwards, catching her heel upon a stone, and fell hard upon the ground. He turned and began walking towards the house. To her own frustration and shame, she burst into tears. He stopped, then turned back to her. Marianne's tears stopped, and she raised her arms in protection against him. He seized them again, but gently this time, and pulled her to her feet. He did not let go, only held her, his hands firm, yet gentle upon her arms. His eyes sparkled as he stared into her face, bright and tormented. His hands slid down her arms, until at last he held her hands in his own. Marianne was paralysed – frightened and irresistibly drawn to him. Then he released her, and she stood, reeling in fright and confusion. He gazed at her a moment, his eyes at once softened and still cold and flint-like. Then he turned away, leaving both her and the horses behind him in the lane.

Marianne returned to the house, and ordered a groom to collect the horses, who, by now, were grazing in the meadow beyond the house.

"Are you quite all right, Miss?" the young servant asked timidly.

"Of course," Marianne replied impatiently. The groom cast his eyes downwards, and she realised that her riding habit was torn and dirty, and that her hair had come unbound. She touched her tangled curls self-consciously. "I fell and the Captain was kind enough to assist me. Now fetch the horses!" And she turned and walked quickly into the house.

Marianne spent much of the afternoon pacing in her room, mulling over the afternoon's events. *How dare he!* she raged, over and over again. *How* dare *he!* She examined her own conduct that day, wondering what had provoked him to such extremities of behaviour.

"Nothing!" she said at last. "I have done nothing to provoke him. It is only his own wicked, impulsive temper that makes him act so." But still, the events of that day ran themselves through her head over and over, giving her no respite. She remembered his roughness, his temper, the white-hot anger in his beguiling, expressive eyes ... and also the warmth of her hands in his, the brightness of his gaze, the warmth of his breath, so close to her face.

"No!" she cried aloud. "I must not allow myself to dwell upon his actions! I must ... I must speak to someone. Someone must punish him." And with this wild thought, she burst forth from the room, and down the stairs, where she almost ran headlong into Louisa.

"Oh! Marianne!" she said with a shocked little laugh. "What have you done to your dress? And you have mud on your cheek – there." And she wiped it off gently with her own handkerchief. "There! Now you must take your dress off and have it washed and mended. But what *did* you do?"

"It's nothing," Marianne said, forcing a smile. "I had a little fall in the lane – nothing at all, I assure you. You are quite right, I will change my clothes." And she allowed her friend to turn her about on the stairs and lead her back to her own chamber. Louisa fussed over her, pulling at the torn fabric of her dress, pulling out twigs and blades of grass from her hair. Marianne succumbed with a forced good humour, wanting only to be alone. At last Louisa moved to the door, and it was all Marianne could do not to sigh in relief. "Call for me if you need anything," Louisa said before she left her friend once again in the solitude of her own chamber. "I'll send someone up for your dress."

"Thank you," Marianne replied, forcing a smile. Louisa left, and she sat upon her bed, feeling helpless and alone. *How could I do anything that might cause dear Louisa any pain?* she wondered desperately. *And who could I possibly tell, in any case?* And she burst into tears once again, feeling very much alone and vulnerable. She spent a long while in her room, crying, and it was with the greatest effort that she managed to stop her tears, rise, and pull of the torn and muddied riding dress.

By seven o'clock, however, Marianne was dressed and composed, her face rubbed clean and her hair bound elegantly upon her head. Her dress, though still mourning black, was simple and elegant, and she tilted her chin proudly upwards. *I will not allow him to affect me,* she thought as she descended to dinner. *I will behave with dignity and good breeding, even if he will not.* She entered the dining room grandly, to find only Mrs Weston seated there.

"Don't you look lovely," Louisa cried, delighted. "What a pity we have no company to see you so fine."

Marianne smiled, softened by her friend's good temper. "What better company could I hope for?" she asked. "Let's have a charming dinner *a deux.*"

"Oh, but Philip will be down presently. At least he will see how handsome you are."

"Ah. Yes. Yes, that will be quite lovely." And Marianne sat down, feeling defeated. Louisa, however, laughed as though Marianne had just told a great joke.

"Oh, yes," she giggled, clapping her hands like a child. "Quite lovely indeed!"

"I am afraid my dear Louisa can be quite silly, Miss Reed." The Captain's voice from the door way startled them both. He moved languidly across the room, and sat down across from Louisa, and next to Marianne. "Pray, do forgive my lateness." And he waved for wine to be brought to the table.

"Oh, you are hardly late, Philip," Louisa exclaimed. "Marianne herself has just arrived."

The Captain smiled, his eyes crackling with an electric light. "Why then," he said in a low, teasing voice. "We must both ask Louisa to forgive us, mustn't we, Miss Reed?"

Marianne felt a hot flush come to her cheeks. She tossed her head and replied shortly, "I will allow you to apologise for the both of us, then."

Louisa laughed again. "Oh, dear, I am afraid you two will never be friends! But you must try for my sake, and little James's, for he and I love both of you so much." Then suddenly, her eyes lit up like those of a child who has a secret to tell. "Oh, I must tell you what James and I have done today! Paul – you know Paul, he is the groom – he has offered us a terrier puppy, and I have accepted! Paul is to bring it from the village tomorrow. Won't James be happy."

The Captain was silent for a moment, then turned with a slight smile to Marianne. "Louisa sometimes – nay, often acts without thinking," he said in a gentle ironic tone. Then he turned to his wife. "Louisa, James is much too young to play with dogs." His voice was quiet and kind as he spoke to her. "They might hurt him. And if we should decide to leave the neighbourhood, how are we to take a dog with us?"

"You worry about such things, Philip! It is only a little dog, and James is not so little now. And why fret about eventualities? If we must leave, we will take the dog with us, or else leave it in Marianne's care. Isn't it so, Marianne?"

Marianne smiled slightly but did not reply. In her enthusiasm, Louisa hardly seemed to notice. Dinner was set before them and Marianne toyed with the food on her plate, only half-listening to her friend's merry chatter, and the Captain's low, practical replies. She allowed her mind to wonder, to wish for the company of her father and mother. She felt that she was being allowed to look in upon a gentle family scene, from which she herself was excluded. She felt very much alone all at once, and a lump formed in her throat.

"You're not eating, Miss Reed," the Captain said all at once. "Are you unwell?"

Marianne forced herself to look up and reply evenly, blinking at the tears that threatened the corners of her eyes. *Will I never stop weeping*, she thought, irritated. "I am quite well, thank you for your concern." There was a momentary lull, and Marianne realised how cold and unsociable her reply had been. For Louisa's sake she smiled and asked. "When is James to receive his puppy?"

"Oh, it won't be for some weeks yet," Louisa said. "They are too small yet to be taken from their mother. Won't it be nice for him to grow big with a puppy to grow with him?" And her happy chatter resumed, allowing Marianne to lapse into silence once more until they all rose from the table at the end of their meal together.

That evening, Marianne and Louisa took a quiet stroll in the gardens. The warm day had faded to a chilly evening, and they were wrapped in their winter shawls. Louisa was quiet; Marianne was by now used to her friend's frequent changes in mood. She would be happy and laughing one moment, then silent and fretful the next. Marianne assumed that the Captain's condescending behaviour was the source of these changes, and she hated him all the more for them.

"Dear, dear Marianne," Louisa said suddenly, grasping her friend's hand and staring earnestly into her face. "You do know that James is the most precious thing to me, do you not?"

"Of course," Marianne replied, trying to laugh. "Why tell me such a thing?"

"Nay, listen," Louisa continued earnestly. "It is more important to me than anything else in the world that he should be brought up properly, that he should have every advantage possible, that he should want for nothing. I would sacrifice everything that I have to ensure his future. You must understand how important that is to me."

"Any mother must feel as you do, I am sure. And surely his father must, too."

Suddenly, Louisa's eyes filled with tears. "Yes. Yes, of course," she replied, wiping them away with the back of her hand. Wordlessly, Marianne offered Louisa her handkerchief. She was completely perplexed by the source of her friend's tears, and knew not what comforts to offer.

"Dear Louisa," she said at last. "Little James must already know that you and Captain Weston love him and would do anything for him."

Louisa smiled through her tears, and took Marianne's arm once again. With a forced brightness, she said, "You are quite right. Philip would protect James from anything. And so would I and so would you. Am I not right?"

"Indeed," Marianne replied. And Louisa giggled slightly, tugging her friend along the path. By the time they returned to the house, she was as bright and impulsive as she had been at dinner, laughing as though she were but a child herself. They sat together next to the warm fire in the drawing room until their hands and feet were sufficiently warmed, allowing Sarah to fuss over them and cover them with blankets and shawls, then mounted the stairs together. They stopped outside Marianne's chamber, and Louisa embraced her friend suddenly and warmly.

"You are a sister to me," she said. "Other than Philip and James, you are the only family I have. I am so glad to have met you!" And before Marianne could reply, she turned and rushed down the hallway, blowing a kiss merrily behind her as she went.

Marianne stood outside her door for a long moment after Louisa had locked herself into the dressing room that had once belonged to Mrs Reed. *She exhausts me*, Marianne reflected, but without malice or impatience. Though she was accustomed to her friend's varying moods, and loved her well enough to humour them, still she did not understand them. Finally she sighed, opening the door to her chamber and stepping into the cool silence inside.

"It must be the effect of living each day with the Captain," she said aloud.

"And what effect is that?" came Weston's own voice from the silence behind her.

Marianne spun about, too shocked and surprised to make a sound.

FIVE

Well, Miss Reed?" the Captain continued, clearly amused by Marianne's shocked silence. "What effect do I have on you?"

Marianne's cheeks flushed as she began to regain her wits. "Why do you think I was speaking of myself?"

Captain Weston released a low, deep chuckle into the darkness. "Ah. Louisa then. Well. Is it a positive effect?"

"What are you doing in my chambers, Captain?"

"Always so direct. I admire that, Miss Reed." As Marianne's eyes adjusted to the dimness of the room, she could see that he was moving languidly towards her. She strode abruptly away and stoked the embers in the hearth. A lazy red blaze caressed the contours of the Captain's face as she turned back towards him.

"Indeed I am. And I wish that you would be so direct. This is my private chamber. Why have you presumed to invade it?"

"I want you to write a letter, my dear Marianne," he replied, sitting down at her writing desk. "I wish you would write to your devoted brother so that we may resolve this uncomfortable debt situation. You see, the income from Barronsgate is hardly what he represented to me. The tenants pay almost no rent at all. I will be here several years before I am repaid."

"And what would you like me to ask him?" Marianne's tone was scathing as she looked at the Captain, seated comfortably at her desk, dictating to her what she must do. She longed to strike out at him, to slap his face. Instead, she stood, stalk-still, looking unerringly upon him as he sat there.

"I would like for you to negotiate for me the sale of Barronsgate."

For a moment, Marianne was too struck to speak. Hardly realising what she did, she sank down upon the bed. "I see," she replied at last. "And to whom is Barronsgate to be sold?"

"To me. I will purchase Barronsgate. I have a small fortune of my own, a very small estate in Somerset, and some interest in the coal mines there. But I am fond of Kent, and I am fond of Barronsgate. I believe I should like to stay. We will subtract Edmond's debts to me, and I believe that I shall be able to purchase this estate, once I have sold my own property. So it is settled, then," he said, rising. "You will write him directly."

Marianne's shock quickly turned to fury. "Oh, yes, it is settled. I will write to him on your command, so that you can turn me out of my own home. Is that how it is to be? You will have me be the instrument of my own demise? You are the cruellest man I have ever set my eyes upon, Captain Weston! And I pity Louisa and little James that they must spend every day in your company! As for me, I would not have it so for the world!" Almost without realising what she did, Marianne had advanced upon Captain Weston until she was standing almost upon his toes. He had risen from his seat, and was staring mutely at her as she yelled at him.

"Marianne–" he began, but she stopped his words as she raised her hand in fury, and struck out at him. He caught her wrist easily in his own hand, and for a moment, Marianne was afraid as she remembered their encounter earlier that day in the lane. Instinctively, she raised her other hand in protection, but he took that in his hand as well.

"Nay, Marianne," he said, and his voice was suddenly gentle, tender almost. "You may wish to strike me, but I would not strike you." He steered her over to the bed and sat her down there, placing her hands softly upon her lap. Then he turned towards the door, and walked softly out of the room. Before he left, however, he turned to face her, and spoke again in the same gentle, firm tone. "I am sorry. But you must write your brother." And then he was gone, and Marianne was sitting dumbfounded upon her bed, unsure of what had just passed between them.

Dear Edmond,
    Much has passed since our dear father died. The neighbours have been all kindness. And your friend Captain Weston has informed me of the debts you have

accumulated. He and his family have taken up residence at Barronsgate in order to save themselves the cost of living at Trent Cottage; I had thought that we might thus discharge your debt to them more easily. The Captain, however, informs me that the income is not what he believed it to be. He has asked me to negotiate with you the sale of Barronsgate. I would like to beg you to find another way to discharge this debt, and to live more prudently in the future. I know that it is not my place to tell you how to conduct yourself, so I will only ask that you assist me in finding a place to live after the Westons have purchased our family home. Please hurry in your reply to
    Your loving sister,
    Marianne Reed.

It was hardly easy for Marianne to compose a letter to her estranged brother under the best circumstances; her situation at Barronsgate and her knowledge of Edmond's own financial straits did not make the communication any easier for her. Marianne fought the urge to berate her brother, to demand that he return home and settle his own affairs, to accuse him of neglecting their father and her – it was with the greatest difficulty that she kept the missive civil and cool. She spent many hours alone in her bedroom, first agonising over the composition of the note, then, finally, in reading and re-reading it, and wondering that she must be the bearer of such news. At long last, she delivered the letter, sealed and unaddressed, into the hands of Barronsgate's would-be owner. Captain Weston obtained intelligence from his former regiment that Captain Reed was stationed in Yorkshire; the letter was therefore sent in that direction, and Marianne attempted to keep up her spirits as she waited for a reply. She avoided the Captain whenever she could, and spent most of her time with Louisa and James. She and Louisa never spoke of their situation, never spoke of the future. In fact, Marianne often wondered whether her friend knew that young Miss Reed was about to be made destitute by young Mrs Weston's ambitious husband. Whether Louisa knew or no, Marianne decided, was irrelevant to their situations; it was out of their hands. Their futures were to be decided by the Captains Weston and Reed. Whatever Mrs Weston and Miss Reed knew or did not know on the subject made little difference to their respective situations. They were friends, and to Marianne, that was all that must matter, at least until Barronsgate was sold. Marianne Reed, once the undisputed mistress of Barronsgate, bore the relative solitude of that house with only the company of Louisa Weston, the woman whose husband would make his wife the mistress of Barronsgate, to console her and to keep her spirits from collapsing altogether.

And as for Louisa, though she was warm and uninhibited in the presence of her family and of Marianne, she suffered from a painful shyness that prevented her from moving much in society, even among the few families that Mr Reed had called his friends. Therefore, after mourners and sympathisers had ceased to visit Barronsgate on behalf of that old gentleman, the house saw fewer visitors than it ever had.

Captain Weston, however, was a popular gentleman in the neighbourhood. In the months following Mr Reed's death, he tried to convince Louisa and Marianne to throw merry parties; here, he met absolute resistance. Louisa's shyness made the idea of such parties terrifying to her, and Marianne, out of respect for her father and Louisa, refused to allow the Captain to have his way in this matter. And soon, he seemed to cease caring altogether about the society that Barronsgate had to offer. Once he had met most of the neighbouring families, he seemed to lose interest in them, one by one, and if he paid many calls of his own upon their neighbours, Marianne did not know it. *Bored of our small acquaintance already*, thought Marianne scornfully. *No doubt he prefers the more lurid company that is to be found in more fashionable places!*

After some, time, however, the ladies of Barronsgate were prevailed upon to begin paying their neighbours afternoon visits, less by the Captain's initial insistence than by Marianne's own sense of what was due those who had been kind to her and her father. Early in the Westons' residence at Barronsgate, before Weston lost interest in his neighbours, these visits occasionally involved all three of the inhabitants of that house. More often, however, Marianne chose to perform her social duties on her own. She pitied Louisa for her shyness, and wished to assist her friend during these awkward moments, but her dislike for the Captain was so intense that she was loath to present herself to the neighbours as a member of his household. She preferred to think of herself as the sole representative of Barronsgate, and the Westons, her indulged guests. It was easier to maintain this illusion by separating herself from their society, even if only for the space of an afternoon; she could then pretend, if only to herself, that their company could be sought out or avoided with equal ease.

Though their kindness and affections for her father softened Marianne towards his friends, she found that she bore very little love for them. She found them a narrow and dull lot, whose main amusement seemed to be gossiping about each other; however, had Weston himself offered this opinion of them to her, she would have defended her neighbours passionately. Most were elderly people, who had been friends of her father, and whose children had found themselves situations as military men, or in London, or as wives of those who had found themselves situations as military men, or in London. Young people were rather a rarity in that neighbourhood. And so, since the Misses Farthington were closest to Marianne in age as well as distance from Barronsgate, it was to this family that Miss Reed paid most of her visits.

"Did you know, my dear Miss Reed – might I not call you Marianne? We have known each other so long that it seems strange that you should not call me Charlotte – did you know that my sister has become engaged since we saw you last? Indeed! She is to marry Mr Christianson! Such a handsome young man, do you not think so?"

"Why, I–"

"Oh, Charlotte! Please!" Antonia Farthington looked imploringly at Marianne. She was a sweet, simple girl with so little personality that Marianne dreaded ever being left alone in a room with her. She was a young woman whose greatest charm was that she was pretty in a soft, fair-haired, blue-eyed manner; though she was very popular with the few gentlemen who resided in the neighbourhood, Marianne found her to be less than a stimulating companion. Her sister

Charlotte's mindless chatter, though it left little room for any sort of conversation, was welcome to Marianne in that it did not force her to search for any sort of intelligent reply.

"My sister pretends she does not like such talk, Marianne. But you see how she smiles, do you not?" Charlotte continued, smiling insipidly.

"I imagine–"

"Of course, you must know what it is to live with such a person. Mrs Weston, I believe, is very much like Antonia. She is such a quiet person! Whatever do you find to talk about?"

"Actually–"

"And yet her husband is so interesting! Don't you find him a fascinating man, Marianne?"

Here, Marianne was caught unawares in that Charlotte had actually paused in her chatter, and was apparently awaiting her guest's reply. She had just taken a mouthful of tea, and almost choked on it as she tried to speak.

"Are you quite all right, Miss Reed?" Antonia asked, patting her anxiously on the back.

"Yes, yes, quite all right," Marianne replied, dabbing at the tears that ran down her cheeks as the hot tea scalded her throat.

"Oh dear, Marianne, what did I say to upset you so?" Charlotte asked, setting down her own teacup.

"Nothing at all, I assure you," Marianne laughed, embarrassed. "I seem to have developed a difficulty in swallowing my tea."

"Indeed!" Charlotte picked up her teacup again, then leaned forward conspiratorially. "So what say you about Captain Weston. Is he not a handsome man?"

"Oh, Charlotte! Do stop!" came Antonia's protest.

Sipping her tea carefully, Marianne said, "I suppose some might find him handsome. He is such a friend of my brother's, as I am of his wife's, that I almost regard him as a brother himself." The lie rolled easily off Marianne's tongue, thought she had to fight back a blush at her own dishonesty.

"Why, that is fortunate, since they are your brother's guests at Barronsgate." Charlotte surveyed her guest over the rim of her teacup.

Unable to lie a second time, Marianne nibbled intently on a biscuit.

"But it is strange that dear Captain Reed himself is not at home to entertain his guests. Does he plan to return to Barronsgate soon?" Marianne scrutinised the elder Miss Farthington. *Does she have designs on Edmond?* she wondered. Like her sister, Charlotte was not an unattractive young woman; however, Marianne suspected that Antonia would be more to Edmond's taste. "No," she replied at last. "Duty keeps him away."

"And yet Captain Weston is at his leisure here in the country. Is that not strange?"

"I'm afraid I don't know," Marianne replied truthfully. "Perhaps the Captain may be called away very soon." *And I hope that he is!*

"What a loss that would be for you!" Charlotte smiled, her blue eyes exaggeratedly large.

"Oh, Charlotte!" Antonia said. Marianne turned to the younger sister. Her face was red, she looked as though she wanted to cry. With a sudden flush of anger, Marianne understood the direction of Charlotte Farthington's insinuations. She forced herself to smile.

"Yes, indeed, it would," she said evenly. "I have grown excessively fond of the family, of Louisa Weston in particular. And my brother is very fond of the Captain, as was my father. They are a very worthy, honourable family."

"Indeed, they are. But pray, who was Louisa Weston before her marriage?"

"I don't know. I have never asked her." *What can that matter to her?* "But I have been made to understand that she is now without parents."

"I am sure it must have been an advantageous marriage for her."

"Oh?" Marianne set down her teacup. "Why do you say that?"

"She seems unused to moving in society. She has not her husband's charm, or his polished manners. Indeed, she is such a shy, awkward creature, I can't imagine that she was a gentlewoman before Captain Weston married her!"

"Charlotte, please!" Antonia seemed near tears. Marianne pitied her, but without any real empathy.

"I assure you," Marianne said with a glacial smile, "that Mrs

Weston is every bit a gentlewoman. She may be shy and reserved, as you say, but I find that infinitely preferable to someone who is forward, insinuating and rude." She rose and nodded stiffly at the young ladies. By now, tears had welled in Antonia's eyes, and her cheeks were blanched, and even Charlotte appeared slightly ashamed and disconcerted. "I thank you for this lovely visit, but I really must be on my way. Good day." And she spun on her heel and stalked out of the room.

Outside, she climbed angrily into the carriage, pounding her fist upon the door as she sat down. "Who are the Farthingtons, anyway?" she muttered aloud, glaring angrily at their drawing room window. "Antonia is only to marry a country doctor, and Charlotte will probably die an old maid! Abominable snobbery!" Her anger continued as long as the lane from the house to the road, but as soon as she had lost sight of the house, she leaned back suddenly and laughed.

"Well," she said aloud. "At least I won't have to inflict another visit to the Misses Farthington upon myself for some time!" She tossed her chin proudly. *And they are silly, ignorant girls if they don't recognise the admirable qualities that Louisa possesses!*

She returned home, dashing from the carriage almost before it had fully stopped, and flew into the house to embrace Louisa warmly.

"Why! You're in a mood!" Louisa said, laughing. "Where have you been?"

"Where I need not go again, and I am glad to be home!" Marianne replied, pulling off her bonnet. "Come now, let us sit by the fire and talk about silly nonsense, or else we shall read together in a lovely, companionable silence!"

"Oh, do go out more often, dear Marianne, if it makes you so happy when you come home!" Louisa laughed, catching Marianne's hands in her own. "Shall I fetch James?"

"Yes, do, then we shall be able to read nothing at all!"

Louisa smiled and bustled up the stairs, and Marianne, laughing, turned towards her father's study, and to the warm fire that she knew the good Sarah would have laid for her. She flung open the doors, and was taken aback to find the Captain already there.

"Captain Weston," she said with what she hoped was a cool flippancy. "What are you doing in here?" And she sat down at the fire, in her father's chair, her back to him.

"I was waiting for you," he said, and she suddenly wished she could see his face. *I can't turn around now*, she thought stubbornly.

"Really? Whatever for?" As she spoke, she strove to keep her voice even and uninterested.

"We have some business to discuss," he said. "Have you heard from your brother?"

"It has been less than a fortnight since I wrote him," she replied, her stomach knotting up. "He has never been a good correspondent, even about important matters."

"Indeed! Irresponsible of him, wouldn't you say?"

Though she herself had thought the same thing countless times, she could not bear to hear the Captain say it. She stood, and spun to face him.

"I would not. I would say that he must be very busy. Perhaps his ship has left the port. He is not a man of leisure, you know. He has other responsibilities."

Captain Weston smiled, and gazed away from her, into the fire. "I would say your brother knows very little about responsibilities," he said quietly.

Marianne's temper flared. "Really, Captain, did you come here to insult me and my family, or is there something else you wished to discuss? Because if there is not, I would like you to quit my sight immediately!"

The Captain's gaze shifted back to Marianne's face. Something like playfulness returned to his own features. "Be careful, Marianne," he said. "You have already seen the effects of your trying to order me about. I am not at your command, my dear."

"Then tell me what it is that you want. I am sure we both want to shorten this interview."

"You are mistaken, my dear Miss Reed! There is nothing that I enjoy more than our conversations." He leaned back a little, a smile playing about the corners of his lips.

Marianne drew in a long breath, and attempted to curb her impatience. *What does he mean, staring at me like that?* She met his mischievous, grey gaze evenly and said, "Captain Weston, kindly begin your *very* important communication, or I will leave this room at once."

"There is the point, Miss Reed. How quickly you have come to understand me! But you mistake my intent entirely, I assure you."

Marianne's irritation was mounting. Weston was now leaning playfully against the bookcase, and she longed to upset it upon him, to knock down all the books upon his exasperating head. "And I assure you, Captain," she snapped, "that I understand you not at all."

There was a long pause before Weston replied. The smile faded from his lips and suddenly, the Captain was all seriousness. His crossed the room and sat down upon the chair before the fire and sat there, brooding, for a moment. *His moods are almost as changeable as his wife's!* "Your brother will not write, I think," he said at last, "and I am determined that Barronsgate shall be mine. I intend to go into London in a very few days to discuss the sale with my banker. But please do not assume that I am insensitive to your situation. I do not intend to turn you out. Continue to consider Barronsgate your own until it suits you to leave."

Marianne felt dizzy and her stomach twisted and knotted painfully. This sudden kindness was more difficult to deal with than his accustomed cruelty and insinuation. Then she took a deep breath and snapped her chin up defiantly. "I do not need your charity, sir. Barronsgate is my home, and it shall remain so until the time that you – you purchase it, *if* that time ever arrives. And if it does, be assured that, on that very day, it will suit me to leave!" And she turned abruptly and almost ran into Louisa, who was standing just inside the doorway. The look of pity and compassion on that woman's face told Marianne that she had been there for some time. Marianne felt confused, felled – she felt that she had suddenly lost her only ally. "Excuse me," she said, pushing her way out of the room, refusing to allow herself to cry before them.

"Marianne? Please let me in," Louisa called timidly through the heavy oak door of her friend's bedchamber. Marianne was tempted to ignore her, to let her go on calling. Instead, she rose grimly from her seat at the window and crossed the room, letting Louisa in. For a moment, Louisa stood awkwardly in the hall for a moment, then stepped uncertainly into Marianne's darkened room. "I'm so sorry – it must have seemed to you that we were – that you were all alone, and – I am sorry, Marianne. I knew nothing of the debts until just now, I assure you. I had thought that we were your guests here, I had no notion that – oh Marianne, you mustn't leave! Where will you go? Please don't leave. Philip will purchase Barronsgate perhaps, but you and I, we must stay just as we are now. Please, Marianne! Please promise me you won't go!" And suddenly, Louisa was sobbing and Marianne was comforting her.

"Hush, hush, Louisa, of course I won't go, not if you want me to stay. Dry your tears, my dear, hush or you'll wake James."

Louisa looked up at Marianne, her eyes round and child-like. "You promise you won't go, then?"

"No, I won't go. I promise." Marianne smiled reassuringly at Louisa, who returned the smile gratefully, then lay down upon the bed, placing her head upon Marianne's lap. Marianne stroked her hair, at once bemused and pitying. *No, indeed, my poor, unpredictable Louisa. I cannot leave if you need me to stay – no matter what I may be asked to endure!*

65

SIX

A few days later, Louisa rose early to bid Captain Weston good-bye as he left for London to conduct his business there. Marianne, too, was awake before six o'clock that morning, and she heard the family stir, but she herself stayed in her chamber until she was sure the Captain had left. She dressed leisurely, bound up her hair, then descended to the dining room for breakfast. There, she found Louisa sitting alone.

"Where is James this morning?" she asked cheerfully, sitting down.

"Sleeping again," Louisa replied, sipping at her tea. "It was awfully early when he rose."

"Indeed!" Marianne paused, then asked, "Louisa, why haven't you gone into town with your husband? Surely it would have been amusing for you."

Her eyes downcast, Louisa replied, "Oh! I don't much like London. You know I'm not very comfortable in society. And I much prefer your company, my dear, to that of strangers."

"But have you no friends in town? Indeed, you must have some cousins or some aunts to visit, mustn't you?"

"No. There is no one in London."

"But what about in other places?" Marianne pressed, seeking Louisa's eyes, and obtaining instead a turned cheek, dropped eyelids. "You must have some friends somewhere!"

"Marianne, don't press me!" Louisa looked up suddenly, her eyes filling with tears as she spoke. "Except you and Philip and James, I have no friends. Why do you wish to remind me that I'm so alone?"

Marianne's chest contracted. She stood, and strode to her friend's chair, taking Louisa's small hands in her own. "I am sorry! I didn't mean to cause you any pain, I only thought that so little company, so

67

little excitement must be tedious to you, I thought you might miss the sort of amusements that can't be had at Barronsgate. Please don't cry, Louisa."

Louisa laughed through her tears. "What a fright we are! Philip leaves and we begin to quarrel! I believe that dear Philip is necessary to our harmony in this house. Wouldn't you say?"

Marianne smiled noncommittally. After a pause she said, "It is a cool day, I think, but let us dress warmly and take a walk in the gardens. What say you – will you walk out with me?"

"Of course. Wait while I go upstairs and change my dress." She embraced Marianne, and bounced up the stairs to her bedroom. Marianne watched her go as she nibbled absently on her bread. *I'll never be able to predict her moods!* she reflected.

Marianne and Louisa spent a happy afternoon walking together in the park, then playing with James in the nursery, dining together, and finally, retiring next to a warm fire in the drawing room. The next day was passed much in the same manner, and the next, and the next. On warmer days, Marianne would ride out onto the estate, and on cooler afternoons, she would read some of her father's favourite books while Louisa read or embroidered or played with little James. Marianne enjoyed her days of leisure and was grateful for Louisa's company, but soon began to grow listless and frustrated. *I need something more to occupy myself,* she thought. With a pang of guilt she realised that since her visit with Charlotte and Edith Farthington, she had neglected some of her father's oldest friends – worthy and dull people who had been kind to her since she was a child. She vowed that she would remedy this neglect.

One clear afternoon in October, Marianne had Paul saddle her horse for the ride. The young man led the horse from the stables, following his mistress silently. His eyes were downcast as he helped her into the saddle, but before handing her the reins, he gazed up at her suddenly.

"Shall I ride along with you Miss? In case you should fall?"

Marianne took the reins in her hand and adjusted her seat. "No, I don't see why I should fall. Thank you, Paul." And she turned her horse down the lane.

"I don't suppose you will," she heard him say as she rode off. She cast a glance over her shoulder. Paul watched her as she led the horse down the lane. She tilted her chin in a gesture of acknowledgement, then turned back to the road, coaxing her horse into a brisk trot.

She spent a perfectly dull afternoon with Mr and Mrs Sinclair, the elderly rector of the parish and his equally elderly wife. Nonetheless, their kindness and fond memories of her father and mother warmed Marianne, so she returned home contented from her visit. Paul accepted her horse's reins from his mistress's gloved hand in silence, his eyes downcast with embarrassment at his earlier rebuffed attempt at chivalry. Marianne smiled kindly at him as she walked past.

"Miss!" he called suddenly. She turned and saw that his cheeks, still pink and smooth, untouched by a man's beard, were flushed with colour.

"Yes, Paul?"

"Will you tell Mrs Weston I have her puppy, if she still wants it."

"Thank you, Paul. I'm sure she will be very pleased. You can bring it by the house later, if you like."

The young man nodded, then rushed off to the stables. Smiling, Marianne walked into the house.

She found Louisa in the sitting room, warming herself alone by the fire.

"Oh! Marianne, you're back! I'm worried you'll catch cold. It will be winter soon, I think. Won't you warm yourself a bit?"

"No, thank you. I'm warmed from the exercise. But where is James? Paul is bringing up his puppy."

"Oh, is he?" Louisa clapped her hands delightedly. *She is so like a child at times!* Marianne thought. "He is just napping – I will wake him."

"Oh, no, let him sleep," said Marianne, intercepting Louisa before she could rush through the door. "He can play with the dog when he wakes, or tomorrow. If you wake him, he will only be cross."

A timid knock at the door made the ladies turn. Paul was standing there, cheeks pink and eyes downcast, holding a squirming, brown and white terrier puppy in his arms.

"Look at him, Marianne!" Louisa cried, rushing across the room and taking the puppy into her own hands. "Let's name him!"

"Thank, you, Paul," Marianne said with a smile, pressing a coin into his callused hand. He nodded shyly and strode away. Marianne turned back to her friend. "Have you picked a name already?"

"No, not yet. But look at him! He is such a brave little creature!" Indeed, the little dog was already making short work of the lace on Louisa's dress. She didn't seem to notice or to mind.

"How about Hercules, then? Or Achilles?"

Louisa finally put the squirming puppy on the floor, and laughed as he ran about the room, exploring every corner. He emerged from behind a chair with a piece of embroidery that Louisa had been working on in his little jaws. "Oh, no!" she exclaimed, clapping her hands together in her exuberance. "He's called Jason, and look, he has just found the Golden Fleece!"

"I see Louisa no more listens to reason than she has any, herself," came a familiar voice from the hall. Captain Weston stepped into the room, and Louisa flew to him, throwing her arms about his neck.

"Philip! You are home so soon!" she cried in delight.

"Indeed I am," he said, prying Louisa loose. "Well, Miss Reed? Do I get no greeting from you?"

"Philip, you know that Marianne is every bit as happy to have you home as I am. It has been very dull here without you." Louisa released the Captain to grasp Marianne's fingers in a muted gesture of excitement. Marianne felt a momentary and confusing pang, of pain almost, as she witnessed the young woman's unrestrained joy at her husband's return.

"Has it?" the Captain asked, surveying the rambunctious little dog. "I would have thought you ladies could amuse yourselves in my absence." And he fixed his maddening, playful eyes upon Marianne's with a conspiratory smile.

"We have, Captain," Marianne said coolly, trying not to be flustered by his gaze. "We have had a wonderfully amusing time since you have been gone."

"Nothing pleases me more," the Captain replied, sitting down before the fire. "Louisa, please fetch me James that I might see whether he hasn't missed me." Kissing Weston's cheek one final time, Louisa left the room, the little dog following her. The Captain and Marianne were alone.

Tightening her fingers into fists, Marianne asked, "Have you concluded your business in the city?"

"I have," he replied shortly, avoiding her gaze.

"And? What news?" she prodded, fighting back the tightness that crept into her voice.

"I have a letter from your brother," he said, drawing forth the missive and handing it to her, still without catching her eyes with his own. "Perhaps you would like to read it in private."

"Please, Captain!" Marianne said haughtily. "Surely its contents are not a secret to you."

"Indeed they are not," he replied, and Marianne could almost believe that she heard a note of pity and compassion in his voice.

Sitting resolutely with her back to the fire, Marianne opened the letter and scanned its contents. A heavy, doomed feeling settled itself around her as she read and re-read. Finally, she folded the letter deliberately, then stood and turned to face the Captain. His eyes flickered upwards to meet his. "I must congratulate you on your purchase Captain," she said, her cheeks flushing with shame and anger as she lost the battle against her tears. "I am sure you will be very happy at Barronsgate, as I have been for many years. My brother writes that he no longer desires to return home, that he is happy to sell it all to you. He has taken rooms at Brighton."

"So near home?" the Captain asked, his voice at once gentle and cruel. "And yet he has not come to visit his dear sister Marianne and his old friend Weston."

Choosing to ignore him, Marianne continued, "He says I may come and live there if I choose."

"Very kind of him," Weston said bitterly.

"Yes," Marianne replied coldly. "You needn't worry, I will not be under your roof for long. But Louisa has asked me to stay. So I will, for a while."

"Marianne," the Captain said, his voice warm and low. "Don't go. I won't turn you out. Stay here – your brother cares nothing for you, he cares nothing for anyone but himself. Barronsgate is as much your home as ever it was." He had stood, and was grasping her hands in his own, crushing the pages of Edmond's letter between her fingers. His face was pained, tortured, even. His eyes, usually so controlled, were wild, electric. Frightened, Marianne pulled away. *He pities me!* she thought, stumbling towards the door, then up the stairs, passing Louisa and James as she went. Marianne had been prepared for cruelty, vulgarity, for Weston's mischievous levity, but not for his pity. She felt confused, crushed, angry almost – she wanted to escape, to run where Weston or his wife could not reach her. She said nothing to Louisa or James, she could hardly see through her tears. Wisely, Louisa let her go.

Marianne locked herself into her room, and cried until her face burned and her head pounded. Then, washing her face at her wash-stand, she straightened her clothes and her hair, and called for Sarah. The young maid appeared, her face pale and frightened as she beheld her distraught mistress.

"Bring me my tea," Marianne said, attempting to regain some measure of control, "and ask Mrs Weston if she will please come and see me."

With a curtsey and a furtive glance at the page in Marianne's hand, kind Sarah was off. Marianne sat down calmly at the window and waited for her to reappear. Finally, there was a timid knock at the door, and both Sarah and Louisa were admitted into the chamber. Marianne waited until Sarah had set out the items for tea and left, closing the door behind her, until she spoke. Finally, with a cup of hot liquid clasped between her icy palms, she began.

"I must congratulate you and your husband, Louisa," she said, attempting to coax a measure of warmth into her voice. "My brother has informed me that Barronsgate will soon be the property of Captain Philip Weston. I want you to know that I hope that you will be very happy here, and that James will grow up strong and inherit this house as he ought." To her own frustration, tears were sliding down her face once again. Louisa sat frozen across from her, her cheeks pale, her eyes wide and frightened as she listened to her friend. "And I am sure that your husband will work to deserve this house, as my brother never did. I will stay here as long as you want me, then I will go and live with Edmond in Brighton." Attempting a laugh, she said, "I will keep house for him there, as I'm sure he never did anything to deserve a wife, so he'll have a sister instead."

"Marianne!" Louisa breathed, her eyes wide. Then she, too, burst into tears, and flung her arms around her friend's neck, almost upsetting the table and spilling the tea as she did so. Finally, the two were quiet, and Louisa assumed her seat once more. Dabbing at her eyes, Louisa said, "It is a pity men needn't work to deserve their sisters as they must to earn a wife!"

"If that were so, what have I done to deserve such a brother?" Marianne asked, forcing a playful smile.

"Oh, no!" Louisa exclaimed earnestly. "I am sure Captain Reed isn't bad! He is your brother, he must be a kind person, perhaps only a bit irresponsible."

"Perhaps," Marianne said neutrally, sipping her tea, once again wondering how well Louisa and Edmond knew each other before Louisa's marriage. The women were silent for a long moment, until Louisa set down her teacup and folded her hands in her lap, suddenly looking very determined.

"Marianne," she said, her voice firm and level, "you must promise me again that you won't leave here."

"I can't stay forever," Marianne began, her eyes downcast.

"Perhaps not, but for some time at least. I need you here. And you need to be here. You can't go to Brighton without knowing what manner of rooms your brother has taken. They might be entirely inappropriate for a young woman. And I have no idea how to run this house, Marianne, and Philip is entirely unacquainted with the tenants and the grounds. Please stay. Don't leave before the spring."

"I can't promise you that," Marianne said, but she was very much impressed by Louisa's well-reasoned appeal. And despite her pride, she couldn't deny to herself that she wanted to stay, to remain in the only home she had ever known. "I will stay for a while," she promised at last. "I won't go until you can manage here on your own." Louisa nodded, pressing her hands together in her lap.

After a time, the ladies of the house descended for dinner, and strode into the dining room arm in arm. They found the Captain already there, waiting for them.

"Is it settled, then?" he asked, rising. "Is Miss Reed to remain with us for some time?"

Marianne's cheeks flushed in annoyance. "Why, Louisa," she said, dropping her friend's arm. "I didn't know you were on your husband's mission."

"I wasn't," Louisa replied, taking her seat calmly. "But Philip and I do share in our desire to have you stay."

"How can I fight such opposition?" Marianne said, her voice determinedly light. "I must bend to your wills."

"And to your own, no doubt," Weston observed.

"Yes," Marianne said, tilting her chin defiantly in his direction. "No doubt." She was beginning to feel assaulted, to regret her assurances to her friend. The dinner began in silence, with Louisa casting her friend furtively apologetic glances from time to time. Finally, the Captain set down his glass, and, levelling his gaze at Marianne, cleared his throat.

"Miss Reed, do you ever visit your tenants?"

"My tenants?" she asked, signalling for more soup.

"Yes, your tenants," Weston said dryly. "Those people who provide you with the means of living this most fortunate lifestyle."

"Philip!" Louisa scolded, blushing.

Marianne smiled coldly. "You should rather say *your* tenants, Captain. And the lifestyle is now yours as well."

"You are quite right, Miss Reed," he continued, apparently oblivious to her attempt at baiting him. "And I ask again, do you ever visit these tenants?"

"I have, at times," she replied neutrally, feeling that an assault was about to begin.

"Good. Then you must begin introducing me to them, if you please."

"How quickly you take an interest in the affairs of this estate!"

"Someone must," the Captain said, once again levelling his cool gaze upon her. "And since its present owner is unwilling, its future owner must fill the void."

"It is to your credit that you are so eager to take the reins." Marianne's anger and loathing was mounting. She was clutching her spoon so tightly that it made an impression in her palm.

"And it will be to your credit if you show yourself willing to assist me." Captain Weston seemed unperturbed by their conversation; his tone was level and composed, and he continued to eat his dinner most calmly.

Louisa giggled nervously. The shrill sound filled the room. "Philip, Marianne! Can't we enjoy this meal together? There will be many more to follow, you know, and we should get into the practice of taking pleasant meals."

"Indeed, we should," the Marianne replied, smiling suddenly and beatifically, hoping to unsettle the Captain. His silence and dropped gaze told her that she had; she spent the rest of the meal in cheerful, meaningless chatter with Louisa.

"Have you any plans tomorrow, Captain?" she asked sweetly, as they prepared to quit the room.

"None," he replied, sounding guarded to her ears.

"Good. Then we shall begin introducing you to some of the tenants." She took Louisa's arm once again, and strolled grandly from the room.

Marianne rose early the next morning, hoping to extend her advantage over the Captain. She dressed simply, tied her hair back in an uncomplicated knot, and descended to find Captain Weston already waiting for her in the dining room.

"I advise you to breakfast quickly," he said, rising as she entered. "Farmers seldom have much leisure time, and they cannot be expected to delay their duties all day for a visit from the mistress."

"Thank you, Captain," Marianne replied, though her stomach growled in hunger. "In fact I do not want any food, I assure you. I am ready." *I won't give him the satisfaction of waiting for me!*

"Good. Paul is waiting outside with my gig."

Marianne strode out of the room and Weston followed, his step at once deferential and mocking to her ears. She quickened her pace so that she might climb into the small carriage without his assistance. Paul stepped nimbly forward and helped her up; she took the reins in her hands and tilted her chin resolutely upward as the Captain took his place next to her. She coaxed the horses forward before he had properly sat down, her lips twitching slightly as he pitched backwards and attempted to regain his balance as they drove down the lane. They rode silently for some time, until a tidy, homely stone house appeared before them.

"This is the Wrights' house," Marianne said as she stopped the carriage. "That is Joseph Wright by the stable, and his wife Anne is at the door."

But the Captain had already dismounted and was strolling over to introduce himself to the bearded young farmer. With a determined smile, Marianne dismounted, tearing the hem of her gown as she did so.

"Good day, Mrs Wright!" she called cheerfully once she had tugged her skirts free, walking briskly towards the house.

"Good day, Miss," that woman replied, tucking the stray hairs nervously under her cap. She stared uncertainly at her visitor for a long moment. Marianne sought dumbly for something to say, hoping that Anne Wright couldn't hear the growls of hunger that stirred from the young lady's middle.

"Like a cup of tea?" the gracious hostess finally asked, wiping her hands on the front of her apron.

"That would be lovely," said Marianne, forcing a smile as much for Weston's benefit as for her hostess's. Mrs Wright disappeared into the house and Marianne cast a resentful glance towards the stables, where Mr Wright and Captain Weston were conversing easily. Sighing, Marianne unfastened her bonnet and followed Mrs Wright into the house.

"Capital people," the Captain said early that afternoon as they travelled back down the lane towards Barronsgate. Their visits had occupied the whole morning, and Marianne was unable to forget that she still hadn't breakfasted. He flicked the reins lazily between his fingers. "Wright's a good man, and young Forster will do well for himself, I think. You seemed to get on well with Lucy Sedley. What was it you were talking of, so long?"

"Swine," Marianne replied, rolling her slippers upon the floor of the gig, attempting to dislodge the dirt from the bottom of the right one. She folded her skirt over her legs, hoping he wouldn't see the muddy patch from the Sedleys' barnyard, where Marianne had tripped on her torn hem and fallen into the dirt. She was almost dizzy with hunger by this time.

"Indeed?" asked the Captain, smiling angelically.

"Yes. I am told that Miss Sedley has quite a touch with young swine. Very fortunate, wouldn't you say?"

"Oh, yes. Quite." Weston turned his face towards the road, and Marianne suspected he was laughing at her. "Here we are," he said at last. He dismounted and offered his hand to Marianne, who ignored it as she stumbled to the ground. Paul started forward from the stables to assist her, but she stopped him with a warning glance.

"It's been a lovely day, Captain," she called over her shoulder, attempting to force a little false cheerfulness into her voice. "We shall have to do this again."

"Indeed, Miss Reed," he replied cordially. "Indeed we must." And as the door closed behind Marianne, she was almost certain that the sound of masculine laughter from outside followed her into the house.

SEVEN

That evening, Captain Weston was unusually talkative and cheerful, and though Louisa shared in his good humour, Marianne could not. She felt herself growing increasingly irritated and restless as she listened to the Westons' meaningless banter about this neighbour and that.

"These people sound lovely," Louisa said brightly. "Marianne, we must go sometime together to pay our respects."

"Indeed! And yet you are completely unwilling to extend that courtesy to the better families of the neighbourhood. Do you not think that they might feel this a slight?"

Louisa blushed to hear her friend's harsh tone, and returned silently to her place by the fireside. The Captain, however, turned to Marianne, his eyes glinting in a manner that made her uneasy.

"It is very kind of you to look out for Louisa, Miss Reed," he said, his voice taking on that note of false cordiality that Marianne knew precipitated an assault. "Very considerate, indeed. We must be careful of what the *better* families think." He paused a moment, and sipped his claret. "And have you told these finer families, Miss Reed, of your imminent move to Brighton?"

"No, I have hardly had the chance." She fought the flush of shame that threatened her fine complexion.

"Really! And yet they have been your family's friends for so long. Pray, why the delay?"

"There has been no delay, Captain. I have simply not had to opportunity to call on my father's friends since we heard of your most fortunate news."

"Because you have spent most of your time visiting your *tenants*." He spat out the word as though it had a bitter taste. "Do you not think that the *better families* might feel this a slight?"

79

Marianne smiled, drawing herself up to meet his challenging gaze. "Thank you so much, my dear Captain Weston. How very kind of you to draw my attention to such neglect. You are always looking out for the well-being of others. So very kind." She stood, her back straight, her eyes locked with his. She met and held his cruel, playful stare until he flicked his gaze over to the fire, where Louisa sat silently, her back to them.

"We are like family, you, Louisa and I, are we not?" he said, his voice at once light and earnest. "We must be on our guards for each other's interests. Mustn't we, Louisa?"

"Come and sit by the fire, Philip, or else you, Marianne," replied Louisa, her face still invisible to them. "Only stop quarrelling, it is so tiresome."

"I fear we must obey," said the Captain, his lips twitching into a subtle smile. "She so seldom commands, it would be too bad to challenge her when she does." Gallantly, he pulled out the chair next to Louisa's. Smiling graciously, Marianne accepted the seat. *You shall not have the better of me, Captain!*

He himself sat down at the desk and began to write letters. The room was silent except for the crackling of the fire. Marianne began to repent her harshness towards her friend. She was, however, unwilling to appear to relent before Weston, so she tried to catch Louisa's eye privately; Louisa would have none of it. *She can be remarkably stubborn at times*, thought Marianne, not without a trace of admiration. At last, Marianne gave up, feeling that the young Mrs Weston must surely forgive her before the morning. She rose and excused herself, and prepared to retire to bed. She embraced Louisa, who responded coolly. Before she left the room, however, the Captain called to her.

"Marianne, it would please me if you would ride out with me tomorrow."

"I thought I might spend the day with your wife," she replied after a brief hesitation.

"Oh, I can spare you quite well, my dear," that lady replied. "Do ride out with Philip, James and I will amuse ourselves at home."

Flushing, Marianne turned to the Captain. "In that case, I would be pleased to ride with you tomorrow." Thus confounded by her

friends the Westons, Marianne climbed the stairs to her bedroom and
retired for the night.

Marianne breakfasted alone the following morning. As she was
sipping her coffee, Sarah entered timidly to inform her young
mistress that Captain Weston was waiting for her by the stables.
Thanking her, Marianne rose and prepared to leave. Sarah, however,
did not move, only shuffled slightly, her eyes downcast.

"Is there something else, Sarah?" Marianne asked, welcoming the
excuse to delay her ride.

"Yes Miss." The young maid paused, but did not look up.
"There's some that says that you and Mr Edmond are to live in
Brighton."

Marianne was unable to reply for a moment. She had hoped to
avoid communicating this news to the servants for some time yet.
Almost unconsciously, she took her seat once again. "Yes, Sarah,"
she said at last. "I fear we are to leave Barronsgate."

"And are the Westons to live here, then, Miss?"

"Yes. Captain Weston has purchased the house and the grounds
from my brother." Marianne drew in her breath. *It must all be out
now*, she decided. "Please send Mrs Frawley to me, Sarah," she said.
Sarah bobbed a curtsey and departed. Only a few minutes later, the
sturdy old housekeeper appeared at the door.

"Miss?" she said, eyeing Marianne shrewdly.

"Mrs Frawley, I would like you to communicate to the other
servants that – that some things must change here at Barronsgate. In
the spring, I am to leave for Brighton to live with my brother. The
Westons will remain at Barronsgate."

"Miss?" Frawley said again, uncomprehendingly.

"Captain Reed has sold Barronsgate, Mrs Frawley. And Captain
Weston has purchased it."

"And will he keep us on, Miss?"

"I don't know," Marianne snapped, annoyed by that woman's
cold pragmatism. "You must ask the Westons." And she left the
housekeeper as she strode out towards the stables. There, she found
that the Captain was indeed waiting for her, and had in his hands the
reins of both her mount and his. Wordlessly, he helped Marianne

onto her horse. They rode for some minutes in silence.

"Are you warm enough, Miss Reed?" he asked finally.

"Yes, thank you. Quite warm." And she wiggled her frozen fingers in her gloves to bring back the feeling to them. And they were quiet again as they rode along. Marianne led Captain Weston along one of her favourite trails, which wound up a hill and at last gave way to a spectacular view of Barronsgate, of Trent Cottage below and finally of the village, nestled snugly within the wooded valley. The Captain reined up his horse and hopped to the ground.

"I had no idea the neighbourhood afforded such beauty, Miss Marianne," he said, offering his hand absently to her.

"Yes. Once you know it, you will find that you never want to leave it," she replied, a lump forming in her throat. She accepted the Captain's help in dismounting and walked a few steps away so that he would not see her emotion.

"You must have been very happy growing up here," he said, placing himself at her side once more.

"Yes, I was." Marianne smiled to cover the sadness and loneliness that threatened to overwhelm her. "And were you a happy child, Captain, growing up in Somerset?"

"You remember everything, Miss Marianne," he said with a chuckle. "Yes, I suppose I was happy. But it was not a happiness that you would understand."

"Because you were a boy and I was a girl? Do not assume that I know nothing of the pastimes of a young boy."

"No, I can imagine what kind of little girl you were. Always playing at boys' games, were you not?" Weston's voice was playful, but without malice. His clear grey eyes were open, disarming.

"Indeed I was," replied Marianne, smiling ruefully and blushing. "It is not that that makes us different."

"Oh? What is it then?"

"That you grew up a gentleman's daughter and I grew up the poor son of a poor farmer."

For a moment, Marianne was unable to speak. She was surprised, and she suddenly felt ashamed of herself, though she couldn't understand why. She dropped her gaze, hiding her face in the brim of her hat. "Oh."

The Captain turned abruptly, and Marianne felt him stiffen as he stood next to her. "Now the lady is repulsed to find herself in the same house as a commoner!" he said, his voice at once cruel and lost, like that of a very little boy. She turned to him and placed her hand on his arm.

"Captain Weston—" she began.

"Don't!" he cried, wrenching his arm away. His face was savage, his eyes now flintlike and fierce. "Please do not pity me, Miss Reed! As you can see I have done very well since then – I earned my Captaincy at Waterloo, I have gained the respect of those that you call the *better families* – I have even bought a gentleman's estate, and I shall resign my Captaincy as soon as that sale is completed. So do not offer me your pity, Miss Marianne Reed, for I want none of it." In his vicious dignity and bitterness, he was both frightening and intensely alluring to Marianne. Hardly knowing what she did, she reached out to him once again. He caught her wrist in his hand, and his grasp was at once gentle and unyielding. She did not know whether he pulled her towards him or whether it was she that drew them together, but all at once, his hand was on her back, his mouth on hers. Her legs felt unsteady beneath her, and her hand found the back of his neck, the warmth of his skin, the softness of his hair. Her fingers curled around it, as she pressed her lips more firmly upon his, feeling their warmth, the simultaneous soft yielding and angry hardness of his mouth. Then suddenly, too soon, he released her and she pulled back with a gasp.

"Marianne," he said hoarsely, his eyes appealing to her with an innocence that stopped her voice in her throat.

She turned and stumbled towards her horse. "I am cold, Captain," she said, mounting unsteadily. "Please. Let us go home." She nudged her horse back down the trail, and Weston followed her silently.

They arrived at the house without speaking another word. They handed their horses to Paul in silence. The Captain followed her into the house with a coolness and a bashfulness that made her uneasy. She stumbled as she attempted to mount the stairs, and he caught her arm, pulling her upright and towards him. She looked down, her face flushing with a sudden warmth, her eyes drawn to his face. He held her a moment longer than was necessary, and even when he released her, she did not move for a moment. Finally, she found the banister with her still-gloved hand, and mounted the stairs with difficulty. The weight of her own body seemed suddenly almost too much to bear, and yet, she was at the top of the staircase almost before she knew it. She stopped there, and turned around, already knowing that the Captain was still there, was still staring at her. She looked at him, and drew in a breath at the sight of his handsome face. His eyes were so cruel, and yet so torn – his gaze filled her with fear and pity. She fought the conflicting instincts that rose within her to run away and lock herself in her own room, and to run to him, to take his face in her hands and to press her mouth to his.

"I will not come down to dinner, I think," she said, her voice almost lost in the heavy air between them. "Will you have Sarah send something warm to my room?" But the Captain did not, would not answer, and so she turned away, walking deliberately and purposely to her own room, where she fell upon her bed, and closed her eyes, and slept deeply and dreamlessly – the slumber of a drunkard or a criminal or an infant.

Gentle voices and gentler fingers woke Marianne some time later. Her bonnet was being pulled away from her tangled hair, her gloves from her clenched hands, her boots from her feet. She blinked in confusion, attempting to focus her eyes in the dim chamber.

"Are you awake, my dear?" asked a soft, familiar voice. Marianne blinked again, and turned her head towards Louisa, who was holding Marianne's crushed bonnet in her hands.

"Are you unwell, Miss?" Sarah asked, pressing her mistress's unlaced boots anxiously to her chest.

"No," Marianne said groggily, sitting up. "Just tired, I suppose. What time is it?"

"A quarter of nine," Louisa replied. "You must have had a very good ride today, you have been asleep since you came back."

"Yes," she said, still unfocused by her slumber. She gazed at Louisa for a moment, and all at once, the afternoon came back to her in a flood of emotion and memory. A lump formed in her throat, and burst forth in the form of a gentle moan of grief and remorse. Almost without realising what she did, she reached for her friend's hand, which still held the ruined bonnet, and sobbed upon it.

"Marianne!" cried Louisa, very much alarmed. "Whatever is wrong? Please tell me, has something horrible happened? Have you heard from your brother? Is he hurt?"

Marianne, however, was unable to answer through her tears, so the good Sarah spoke for her. "She has received no letters, Mrs Louisa. She is likely feeling the loss of her home, is all. Let her cry – she will feel better in the morning."

And so the three women fell silent, except for the sound of Marianne's grief. *Forgive me, Louisa*, she pleaded silently, *forgive me for what I have done to you and James today!*

Gradually, Marianne's tears subsided, and Louisa wisely left the room in silence, allowing Sarah to tend to her mistress in private. Marianne herself was unable to speak at her friend's departure, and stared at the door long after it was closed by the gentle, kind Mrs Weston.

"Don't worry, Miss," Sarah said soothingly. "The Westons are kind people. They would not make you leave if you wanted to stay. Your father provided you with a little income of your own – perhaps you could pay some of it to them, in exchange for your keep here at Barronsgate."

"No," Marianne replied blandly. "I will stay until spring because Mrs Weston wishes it. After that, I will come to Barronsgate no more."

"Ay me! And you would not miss it?"

"Indeed, I am sure I will, just as I miss my mother and my father. But regrets solve nothing, Sarah, and it does no good to wish for things that have been taken from you, once they are gone. Now, please, leave me. Stir up the fire before you go, I won't want you for the rest of the evening."

Sarah obeyed her mistress in silence, and once she was gone, Marianne sat near the warm embers in the hearth, her back to the shadows and gloom in the corners of her chamber. She unbound her tangled hair and began to comb it, tugging absently at the curls and knots.

A moment of weakness and of pity, she said to herself, unable to forget the taste of his mouth, the smell of his breath. *We pitied each other, and it made us lose our senses. It won't happen again. It must not happen again.* And she pressed her hand to her mouth for a moment, as though to stamp his kiss there, then rubbed at her lips, determined to wipe it away.

EIGHT

Though the weather had grown unseasonably chilly, Marianne soon began to take long walks in the gardens. She rebuffed Louisa's entreaties that they should walk out together, or spend afternoons reading together or playing with James. Her guilt almost sickened her every time she saw the confused, hurt look in her friend's eyes, but she could not allow herself to pretend that her betrayal of the gentle, ingenuous woman had not occurred. *I do not deserve the affection of such a woman!* she thought to herself over and over again. So, day after day, she would wrap herself in her warmest cloaks and venture out onto the grounds and walk about in the damp, gloomy cold, torturing herself with her own guilt and shame.

As for Weston, he seemed at once to seek her out and to avoid her. He took his meals at odd times, or in his own chamber, unless he knew that she would not be dining with the family. Yet if she went out riding, he would pass by the stables as she rode out or returned home. If she read in her father's study, he would come in silently once or twice to find some writing paper or a book or one of little James's toys. And when she walked out into the gardens, she would find him hovering about the entrance of the house when she returned home. And he would do all this almost without a word – he would not stop her or speak to her, merely nod as one would on passing an acquaintance in a very busy place. And she noticed all this also without a word, and almost without realising it, she began to depend upon his silent presence, to expect his shy, guarded gaze every time they met.

And so, one chilly, damp afternoon as she walked through the gardens, she heard a footfall behind her and she turned, expecting to find him there, unspeaking and pretending that this intersection of their paths was an accident. Instead, she was surprised to find the shy, young groom on the path.

"Paul! Has someone come to visit?"

"No, Miss," he replied, falling shyly into step next to her. They walked in silence for some time, until Marianne began to feel impatient and annoyed at his intrusion.

"Is there something you would say, Paul?"

"Yes, Miss," he said, and was silent for another moment.

"Well?"

"I've been in your family's service since I was born, Miss – most of us have."

Marianne offered what she hoped was a motherly smile. "I understand. You are worried what will happen after the Westons take over Barronsgate."

"No, Miss Reed."

"No? Then what is it, Paul?"

Paul did not answer at once. His eyes were downcast, and he seemed to be struggling to find the right words. "We're worried about you, Miss. That is, you seem unhappy. And we were wondering if you should stay here so long."

"I see," Marianne replied, her voice taking on an icy edge. "And by *we* you mean the other servants, do you?"

"Yes, Miss – that is, I mean Sarah and me."

"And what affair is it of yours or of Sarah's whether or no I am *unhappy?*"

"None, Miss," the boy replied, blushing deeply, and allowing his step to fall slightly behind hers. Marianne took the advantage, keeping her pace brisk and her tone clipped.

"And I will thank you to remember that. It is my own affair, and I will decide where I will best live," Marianne said, then stopped, and turned suddenly to look at him. He was clearly miserable, his head bowed, his cheeks bright red, and his eyes dampening with unshed tears. "That is all, Paul."

He turned to go, and a pang of pity and gratitude touched Marianne's heart. She was suddenly ashamed of her coldness. "Paul," she called. He stopped and turned, looking to her eyes very much like a beaten dog. "Thank you for your concern. But it is not necessary." He nodded, and straightened his shoulders slightly before he walked back towards the house and the stables. Marianne could not help but smile slightly to herself as she turned and continued her walk with renewed vigour.

She returned home late that afternoon to find Louisa taking her tea alone in the sitting room. She stood at the doorway for a moment, surveying the peaceful scene before her – the warmth of the fire, the familiar furniture, and the figure of the only woman that Marianne could sincerely call a friend. Suddenly, Marianne felt very lonely, and longed to be a part of the tranquillity before her. She stepped quietly into the room, and felt suddenly and overwhelmingly grateful when her friend looked up towards her.

"How was your walk, Marianne?" Louisa asked with a quiet smile.

"It was … very refreshing, thank you," she replied, sitting opposite her friend. "What have you ordered for tonight's meal?"

"Oh – Philip has been out shooting. I thought we should have some of his pheasants. I suppose you will take yours in your room again."

"No, if you don't mind, I imagine that I shall intrude on your dining room."

"Oh! It is not my dining room!" Louisa replied, looking alarmed.

"Yes, it is," Marianne said, gently and almost without pain. "It is your house and your dining room. Your husband has bought you a fine home. You and James will be very happy here, I promise you."

Louisa's eyes filled with tears. "Marianne! You do not know—"

"Yes, I believe she does know how happy you are, my dear," came the Captain's voice from the doorway. "She knows because she knows you, almost as I do."

Furtively, Louisa wiped at a stray tear. "Did you shoot many birds today, Philip?"

"None, I'm afraid," he replied, moving closer to the fire. "I went out for a ride. And how have you ladies spent your day?"

"Why, Marianne went out walking, of course, and I received a visit this morning from the Misses Farthington," Louisa recounted calmly, as though these activities had become a part of her everyday routine.

"Indeed!" replied Marianne, very much surprised.

"Yes. They arrived not long after you left on your walk. They were very disappointed to have missed you."

"I imagine they were," Marianne said wryly.

"They seem to be very pleasant girls, I think, although perhaps the elder one is somewhat...." Louisa trailed off, blushing.

"Yes, I think I know what you mean," Marianne replied, laughing. "And I'm sure she was very disappointed not to see me in my fallen state." She felt no pang of regret, only a sort of malicious irony as she imagined Charlotte's dismay at the news of the sale of Barronsgate.

"Miss Marianne, you speak very uncharitably of one of your *better families.*" Weston was leaning against Louisa's chair, his expression at once challenging and amused.

"You are right, Captain, I do," said Marianne, smiling slightly at him. *Am I mistaken, or is he smiling back?* She thought that she had seen an expression of real sympathy and sincere amusement in his face. But Weston was already moving away, and the subtleties of his features were lost to her.

The room was silent for a moment, and Louisa finally said, "I think I shall go and see if James is not yet awake. I will see you both at supper." And with a quick smile at Marianne, she was gone.

The room was silent for a long moment, but Marianne sensed that much of the strange tension that had endured between herself and Weston these many weeks was almost completely gone.

"Will Edmond stay in Brighton for Christmas, do you think?" the Captain asked at last.

"I believe he will," replied Marianne. And she herself was silent for a long moment. "And I believe I must join him."

"What!" The Captain spun about, and expression of complete surprise upon his face. Marianne almost laughed. *So you can be taken aback after all!* "I thought you were to stay with us until the spring!"

"And so I shall, I think," she said softly. "But I have not seen Edmond more than twice these five years at least. And if I am to keep house for him, I believe we must reacquaint ourselves."

"It is not necessary, you know. You may stay here as long as you wish." Weston regained his composure, and though his tone was light, Marianne sensed a real sincerity in it. She looked at him, and she knew that they were both, at that moment, thinking of the day that they had ridden out together, when they had....

"Yes, Captain Weston," she said firmly, but without looking at him. "I believe it is necessary."

He did not reply. They sat in silence for a moment before she rose from her chair. "I will see you at supper," she said. He bowed gracefully as she left the room.

She walked to the stairs, and placed her hand upon the rail. Suddenly, she felt as though a very heavy weight had been placed upon her. She climbed the stairs very slowly, and walked to her chamber to change for supper.

"Don't you like the soup, Marianne?" Louisa asked, eyeing her friend with concern.

"No, no, it's very good." Marianne sighed, and summoned up the courage to tell Louisa about her imminent journey.

"I would have thought that your walk today would have made you very hungry."

Marianne laid down her spoon and sighed. "Perhaps it would have, Louisa, only...." Marianne's voice caught, and she found it difficult to continue. "Only I have some news I must share with you."

"And is this news so bad it affects your appetite?" Louisa asked with concern.

"It is not bad news, it only reminds me of what must follow. Of what my future must someday be." Marianne looked up and saw that Captain Weston was staring fixedly at his plate, unwilling to meet her eyes or Louisa's. "I am afraid that I must leave you for Christmas. I must go to see Edmond in Brighton."

"But Marianne! You promised you would stay until the spring!" Louisa cried, and Marianne could not help but smile a little, despite her sadness and regret. *She sounds so much like a disappointed little girl!*

"And I don't intend to break my promise, only I feel that I must see my brother before I am to live with him. I must see where he

91

lives, and what I must expect in the spring."

"Of course you must," replied Louisa with a visible attempt at bravery. "Only we will miss you while you are gone, won't we, Philip?"

"Oh, I believe we must get on tolerably well," Weston replied blandly, still staring into his soup. "After all, we did not suffer before we knew Miss Reed."

"He will not admit it, but he will miss you as I will, and as James will," said Louisa earnestly. Marianne wished that the Captain would lift his eyes so that she could guess at what he was thinking. *Perhaps he is glad to get rid of me! Perhaps he sees me as an annoyance and a temptation.* She suddenly felt tired and quarrelsome.

"Oh indeed, I am sure he is eager to assert himself as master of Barronsgate," she said blithely. "Perhaps he feels that the servants do not obey him so quickly as they should while I am still here."

The Captain looked up at last, and his eyes sparkled with that challenging animosity that Marianne had come to know so well. Despite herself, she felt a shiver of eagerness run along her spine. "Miss Reed, I assure you that if I felt that was the case, I would dismiss them all at once."

"Really! You have such a high regard for your tenants, but you would be rid of the servants so easily. Pray, explain the distinction in your regard, sir." She blinked innocently, not allowing a smile to tug at her lips.

"I give every man his due regard, no matter his station. But I expect every man to perform the duties of his station, and to earn my regard. And if he does not perform his duties, he forfeits his station." His voice was even, rehearsed, and yet tension played about the muscles in his jaw.

"It is very fortunate that such a fair man as you are is the judge of other men's worthiness. But I wonder, Captain Weston, who is to be the judge of you? Who dismisses you if you do not perform your duties?"

The Captain tossed his napkin unceremoniously upon the table and rose to leave. "Louisa, Miss Reed, you will excuse me, but I am no longer hungry," he said before stalking out of the room. After he had left, Marianne could not repress her laughter.

"Oh, Louisa, I believe that I will miss arguing with your husband when I am gone!" she cried.

"I wish you would not provoke him, Marianne," replied Louisa calmly, still eating her soup. "I do not know anyone who affects his moods as you do."

"Then I will take that as a compliment," said Marianne, and began to eat her soup with a renewed appetite.

From her seat in the saddle, Marianne smiled down at her friend. It was a fine morning, and Marianne was in fine spirits. The same, however, could not be said of Louisa.

"I am no great horsewoman, Marianne," she whined, shying away from the fine animals.

"Come, Louisa. There is no gentler horse in the world than Rosinante. She was my father's favourite. Please ride out with me. I know you will enjoy yourself."

"Can we not walk out? I am sure it cannot be as far as that!" Louisa eyed the gentle old mare as though it were a rampant wild stallion. Marianne sighed patiently.

"Indeed it is not, by horse," she said firmly. "Now, let Paul help you into the saddle."

Reluctantly, Louisa obeyed, and the ladies were off. The sun shone brightly upon them, dulling the chill in the air, and Marianne was elated to have her friend riding beside her. She led them down the familiar trail, smiling a little to herself when Louisa shifted awkwardly in the saddle. "Are you so uncomfortable as that?" she asked kindly.

"No, I suppose not. It is only a year or two since I learned to ride," replied Louisa quietly, and she looked so unhappy that Marianne began to repent her plans.

"It is not much further, I promise you. And then we shall rest." She turned her horse along the little used path, so familiar to her, and her heart quickened slightly as the horses began their gentle climb up the hill. The clearing appeared before them, and Marianne fought the sudden urge to turn her horse back towards Barronsgate. Instead, she smiled brightly and led Louisa to the grassy plateau, dismounted, and helped her friend to do the same.

"Oh!" the little woman breathed, her eyes wide as they surveyed the valley below. "Is that Trent Cottage? And the village down below!"

"It is. Do you like it here?"

"It is beautiful!" And Louisa took Marianne's hands in her own and gazed mutely at the beauty that surrounded them. The women remained there for a long moment, content and silent. *There!* Marianne thought with satisfaction. *There are no demons here.*

And so, the remaining weeks of fall drifted away quietly for Marianne. She spent the cool days inside with Louisa and little James, and even managed to coax Louisa onto a horse twice more, to return to that wooded hill that Marianne had so determinedly exorcised. Edmond wrote to tell his sister that he would expect her company in December. The offhanded, detached tone of the epistle stung Marianne, but for Louisa's benefit, she nonetheless bustled with pretend excitement at the prospect of her visit.

"Brighton is such a gay place this time of year," she said over breakfast. "It is not London, to be sure, but after so much solitude in the country, one does begin to crave some society and pleasure."

"To be sure," replied Louisa quietly.

"And I shall not be away for long – a fortnight, or a month perhaps. You will hardly even know I am gone."

"Oh, to be sure, I shall not miss you at all. In fact, I can hardly wait for you to be gone."

Marianne blinked once or twice before she realised that Louisa was laughing behind her hands. With a rueful chuckle, she replied, "Yes indeed. And your society is so very tedious, I wish that I were leaving this very morning!"

Louisa laughed in return. The pair ate their breakfast in companionable silence until, with a sad-looking smile playing at the edge of her lips, Mrs Weston said to her friend Miss Reed, "Marianne, I know how little you desire this visit with your brother. You cannot fool me, you know. Stay, I beg you. Do not go to Brighton."

Forcing herself to smile, Marianne replied, "I must go, I am afraid, for I must know the man whose house I am to keep in the spring. I am afraid he is quite a stranger to me, brother or no."

"Then do not keep house for him! He does very well on his own, I am sure. And Barronsgate is your home – stay here. I assure you, it is much too big for Philip and James and me. If your pride will not allow Philip to maintain you, offer to pay him from the money your father left you!"

"Ah. I see that you and Sarah have been conspiring against me."

Louisa chuckled. "You are right, I'm afraid. But it's sound advice, don't you think?"

Marianne sighed, and her own smile faded. "Yes, but – I cannot stay. I am sorry – I can't say why, but I simply cannot stay. But we shall always be friends – nay, sisters. I promise you that."

Her eyes filling with tears, Louisa replied, "Yes, Marianne. I want nothing more than to be your sister." And she embraced her friend swiftly and fiercely, and left the room before Marianne could utter another word.

All too soon, the morning that Marianne had appointed for her departure was upon her. She rose early and breakfasted, and could not help but be touched when all three of the Westons descended to join her in the dining room.

"It is not yet seven o'clock!" she exclaimed, setting down her cup. "Had you not better be in bed?"

"Indeed, we wouldn't miss your departure!" Louisa cried, grasping her friend's hand. But Marianne's attention was upon the Captain, who was holding a squirming James in his arms. He caught Marianne's eye, and she was almost certain that she saw a blush touch his cheek. But just then, the youngest Weston let out a loud wail that forced the Captain to hand off his charge to Louisa, and Marianne was not sure at all what had just passed between them. Although she had hardly seen him at all that autumn, she believed that the tension and awkwardness between them had almost dissipated; however, there were moments at which she would have gladly given everything that she had to know his thoughts.

"The chaise is ready," he said presently, from his vantage point by the window.

Marianne rose, fighting the sinking sensation in her breast. "Are you quite sure that you can spare it, Captain?" she asked. "I wouldn't mind travelling post."

The Captain shook his head at the idea of a rented carriage, filled with strangers perhaps. "It isn't safe, Miss Reed," he replied without looking at her.

"Paul and Sarah will be with me – I would be quite safe, I'm sure of it," Marianne said, trying to glimpse his eyes, to guess what he was thinking at that exact minute.

"Nonsense," he said blandly, still not looking at her. "The chaise and the horses are still yours, or your brother's at any rate. There is no reason for you to travel post-chaise when you have one of your own at your disposal."

"Marianne! You wouldn't be comfortable! And we never use the chaise – Philip's gig does very well!" Louisa enjoined, rising. "Now, do stop being so silly, and be on your way before we change our minds and do not allow you to go." And she embraced her friend, and almost pushed her out the door and into the carriage, where Sarah was already waiting.

"Write me as often as you can," Louisa begged, blinking through her tears. She grabbed Marianne's hand through the carriage window. "And promise you won't be away long."

Marianne tightened her gloved fingers around the bare, little hand. "You'll hardly miss me at all." Louisa nodded tearfully, and fled back into the house.

Marianne smiled slightly and turned to the Captain. "You, however," she said with a light playfulness that she did not feel, "I charge you to miss me a great deal." The Captain looked up suddenly and caught her eyes with an expression that seemed to dissipate all lightness from the air between them.

"Safe journey, Miss Reed," was all that he said, and she hardly had the time to nod politely in reply before he had spun on his heel and strode back into the house. Marianne leaned back upon the seat, feeling as though she had had her breath knocked from her. When the chaise jerked into motion, she hardly noticed at all, and as they rode down the lane, she watched Barronsgate recede, feeling almost that she was standing still, and that her home was moving away from her.

96

NINE

The journey to Brighton was a quiet one. The chaise stopped frequently, spending the night in a simple, tidy inn, and leaving after breakfast the following morning. The weather was fair – neither too warm, nor too damp – and the roads were good. Sarah slept much of the way, her head nodding upon the side of the carriage, a circumstance for which Marianne was grateful. Her thoughts weighed heavily upon her, and she did not wish for even the kindest of interruptions. It occurred to her that she hardly knew her brother – when she tried to conjure up a picture of his face, she found that the only image that came to her mind was of his red coat – the militia regimentals that he had been wearing the last time she had seen him. Worse yet, Weston's face was the one that rounded out that image each time she tried to recall the particulars of Edmond's features.

Marianne spent much of the journey thinking of Barronsgate, and of those who were soon to possess it. She longed to tell Paul to turn the carriage back, to take her home. But almost before she knew it, the busy streets of Brighton were before her. It had been over a year since her last trip to London, and after so much solitude and quiet country life, the noise and animation of the seaside city were almost too much for her. An intense headache gripped her before they were in town five minutes. The horses and carriages rushing past hers, the loud, innumerable voices and noises, and even the rocking of her own chaise as it rattled over the cobbled streets made travel through the city so insupportable to her that she was just about to call for Paul to stop the carriage when it pulled to a halt on its own.

"I believe this is the place, Miss," whispered Sarah.

Marianne blinked and looked about. The street was not unpleasant, its buildings not as shabby as she had feared Edmond's new home might be. She stumbled out of the carriage with Paul's help and, squaring her shoulders, she marched up the stairs of a narrow, respectable-looking red brick home. It suddenly occurred to her that she might be about to meet Mrs Reed. *Wouldn't it be like Edmond to marry and tell no one!*

A bland-looking young man in slightly faded livery answered the door.

"Captain Reed, please," said Marianne, hoping for a soft chair and hot tea before too long.

"The Captain is from home, Miss," the servant replied, blinking impassively.

"Marianne Reed, the Captain's sister," she replied haughtily. "He is expecting me."

"Is he," the infuriating young man replied, looking past her at the carriage. "Very well then. Come in, I will see to your carriage and your bags."

Marianne stepped past him without a word of thanks and untied her bonnet, handing it to Sarah. She felt peevish and tired, and had little patience for her brother's servant. "Where is the Captain?" she asked.

"He is from home, Miss."

"Yes, so you said. And when will he not be from home?"

"Perhaps later, Miss. Shall I show you to the parlour?" the servant asked without any apparent enthusiasm.

"Yes, do. And bring in the tea immediately, please."

With a surly nod of the head, the young man opened a door to his left and disappeared in the opposite direction. Marianne walked into the dusty parlour and sat down gratefully before a dying fire. Sarah moved forward to stir the embers, but Marianne stopped her.

"No, Sarah, there is no need. But please, see if you can't find out where we are to sleep." Marianne attempted a smile and Sarah, with a worried nod, bustled away, leaving her mistress to rest her eyes for a moment alone. She closed her eyes and was just drifting off when the young servant who had answered the door appeared with the tea things. Marianne surveyed him as she took her first soothing sip.

"Are you the only servant here?" she asked.

"There is also the cook, and one maid," he replied.

"And you do not know when my brother is?"

"No, Miss."

"And he did not tell you I was coming?"

"No, Miss."

Marianne sighed. She motioned for him to leave her, and was left on her own once again. She finished her tea without any appetite and lay down on a slightly shabby-looking sofa for a nap. Sarah came down to tell her mistress that a bed chamber was ready, and to cover her with a shawl.

"Wake me when Edmond gets home," Marianne murmured as she drifted into sleep.

Some time later, Sarah shook her mistress awake. Marianne blinked for a moment, trying to remember where she was. Her neck ached, and she sorely wished for a bath. She wondered briefly why Louisa hadn't yet come to fetch her for supper. Then the day's journey washed back upon her and she sat up, blinking. "Is Edmond returned?" she asked, pushing her fingers through her tangled hair.

"No, Miss Marianne," the kind maid replied gently. "We thought you might be hungry. Will you take something to eat?"

Marianne nodded and rose groggily to her feet. She gazed down at her rumpled grey travelling dress. "I don't imagine there is any point in changing for supper, is there?"

"I suppose not, Miss."

"All right, then. Help me fix my hair and show me where the dining room is," she said wearily, rubbing her tired eyes.

Marianne ate a solitary, unappetising meal, then ascended to a large, bare-looking room and a strange bed for the night. And despite her attempts at courage and stoicism, she shed a few tears upon her strange pillow on that night, her first in Brighton.

She woke early the next morning, but did not rise. She lay in the strange bed, listening to the sounds of the city outside, and to the silence inside the house. Then she heard the familiar quiet bustle of Sarah's duties. She sat up reluctantly to find that her headache still had not released her. She pressed the palm of her hand to her forehead and squeezed her eyes shut, willing the pain away. Then, slowly, determinedly, she rose from her bed and rang for Sarah to help her to dress. She refused to allow herself to wonder where her brother was, or whether he had forgotten her; instead, she reminded herself firmly that she would enjoy the pleasures that Brighton had to offer her, and spend her evenings in the company of family for the first time since her father died. She willed herself into a grim sort of cheerfulness as she dressed. Then Sarah came in and fixed her mistress's hair, and Marianne descended to breakfast.

As she expected, she ate alone, and tried not to be too disappointed, then returned to the sitting room. On her way, she met the bland, young servant, whom Sarah had identified to her as Collins. She stopped him.

"Is the Captain returned home?" she asked.

"Yes, Miss," said Collins, barely pausing.

"And does he know I am arrived?" Marianne persisted.

"Yes, Miss. I told him last night."

"When can I expect to see him?"

Collins shrugged indifferently. "He does not often rise before ten."

Marianne glanced at the clock in the hall – it was barely past eight. She sighed. "Very well. Sarah and I will go for a walk, I suppose. Please tell him I will see him early this afternoon."

Collins nodded and continued on his way; Marianne summoned her maid and donned her shawl and bonnet without enthusiasm. Together, they strolled out into the crowded streets, stopping perfunctorily to admire shops and churches, and the sea-bathing machines along the water. Marianne could not help but enjoy the exercise, and her mood lifted slightly. *If only Louisa were here, Brighton would be so much more pleasant!* She reflected that the amusements of a busy society would do young Mrs Weston a great deal of good. As they walked along, Marianne remembered her friend's shyness and awkwardness at their first meeting at Trent Cottage; since then Louisa had not much improved in company. She was always uncomfortable whenever she encountered the more genteel and fashionable members of Barronsgate's rather small neighbourhood. *But she did see Edith and Charlotte Farthington on her own*, Marianne reminded herself. *Perhaps she only needs to grow more accustomed to society before she can enjoy it.* She was rather young, and could not have been much in fashionable company before she married Captain Weston. Her shyness may have been simply that of a young girl who had not yet mastered the forms and rituals of a fashionable milieu. Marianne reflected that several months in Brighton or London would remedy that, and Louisa's natural grace and bright, happy nature would quickly overcome the awkward, timid Mrs Weston that Marianne had first met.

She returned to Edmond's home, and climbed the steps with a slight feeling of dread. She entered, and a flutter of nervousness at seeing her brother caused her to muddle the ribbons of her bonnet into a horrible knot. She could scarcely stand still as Sarah attempted to undo it. Then, from behind, she heard a deep voice that was at once strange and familiar.

"Gad, what a lady you've become, Mary!"

Marianne spun around. There was Edmond, looking very much the dandy in his stylish clothes, smiling at her. All at once, his selfishness and irresponsibility, and all the years of his absence did not matter to her – she flew to her brother as though she were only a child of ten, her arms around his neck in a juvenile embrace.

"Edmond! How well you look! But why are you not in your regimentals?" she cried.

Captain Reed laughed, prying his sister loose. "You do not think I wear them all the time," he asked, undoing the knot in her bonnet. "Now stop and hold still and let me look at you!"

Marianne stepped back, suddenly self-conscious while her brother surveyed her with mock-seriousness. "Not bad," he murmured. "Yes, indeed," he said at last, "I shall have no trouble finding you a husband in Brighton – a rich, old Colonel at the very least."

"Edmond, don't!" she admonished, suddenly and inexplicably ashamed. She took him by the hand and led him into the sitting room. "No more nonsense, please, but tell me what you have been doing these five years. Lord, it's been so long!"

"I've been in the Indies for most of them," he replied grandly, taking a seat by the window. "Quite exciting, really – tiger hunts and all that."

Marianne frowned, suddenly serious. "But why did you not come back for Father's funeral, or Mother's?"

"Couldn't be helped, I'm afraid," he said, accepting the hot chocolate and biscuits that Collins brought to him silently. "Have you breakfasted?" Marianne nodded, and Edmond continued. "When I heard of Mother's death, I was on a ship headed to Ceylon, and when father died, my regiment was just departing from the West Indies. I would never have made it to Barronsgate in time, so I stayed where I was."

Marianne frowned into the fire. Already, her irritation with her brother, temporarily abated by the joy of their reunion, was returning.

"But let's talk of pleasanter things," Edmond continued, oblivious to his sister's mood. "I've taken a box for us at the opera. You'll not be wearing mourning the whole visit, will you?" he asked, eyeing her sombre grey dress.

"No," she replied, looking at his own lively attire. "I have brought some other clothes with me."

"Good. Very good. You'll meet my friend Colonel O'Donnel. His wife is a pretty, lively young thing, I'm sure you'll be good friends."

Marianne attempted to smile. Edmond, encouraged by the gesture, prattled on about his fellow officers, completely unaware that his sister and sole audience was not listening. Instead, she was looking at his bright, expensive clothes, his easy, indolent manner, and comparing his behaviour with another Captain that she knew. She realised with pain that the comparison was not in her brother's favour.

Marianne and Edmond dined together that evening; Edmond continued his lively prattle about the society at Brighton, and Marianne attempted to listen. After they had eaten, she rose to her room to dress for the evening's entertainments. She donned her favourite plum-coloured gown, allowed Sarah to curl and primp her hair, then descended to meet her brother.

"Don't you look well!" Captain Reed exclaimed. "Tomorrow, we will send you out to purchase some new gowns, so that you may be every bit as fashionable as the ladies of Brighton!"

Marianne smiled wryly. "And what is the matter with this gown?"

"Nothing at all, Mary, only it is not so fine as those the fashionable ladies wear. I suppose it does very well in the country."

"Indeed, it does," said Marianne, taking her brother's arm and biting her lip.

"You must speak to Mrs O'Donnel. I am sure she knows best where to purchase such baubles. She's quite lovely, you will see. A very fashionable young woman. You'll get along famously." He led her down the stairs and handed her into the carriage, which, Marianne noticed with relief, was in Paul's care. Edmond climbed into the carriage after his sister and leaned forward conspiratorially. "Quite a provincial fellow, your little groom. Do you intend to bring him with you in the spring?"

"Yes, Edmond, I do," Marianne replied irritably. "I trust him – he is extremely valuable to me. I will bring Sarah as well."

"Yes, I suppose you must," Edmond said offhandedly. "A lady needs her maid, doesn't she? I don't suppose my Abigail will do – she can't do much else than clean and send out the laundry. Certainly wouldn't be able to pin up your hair, or help you dress, or such things. Though I suppose they will be devilishly expensive to maintain, all these servants of yours."

"Oh, you needn't worry. I will save where I can. Perhaps I had better not buy many new gowns while I am here."

"No, perhaps not," Edmond agreed. Marianne smiled acridly.

They met Colonel and Mrs O'Donnel at the opera house, and Edmond greeted his friends with pleasure. O'Donnel himself was a pleasant enough man, in his early forties perhaps, with a ruddy, wind-worn complexion, and a hint of Irish in his speech. His wife was perhaps two or three years Marianne's senior – a handsome, lively woman with thick blond curls and a ready laugh which Marianne found a little too loud. Her dress was indeed fashionable, and her hands, ears and throat were decorated with several large, brightly-shining and expensive-looking jewels. She laughed and flirted with both Edmond and her husband in a manner that made Marianne blush.

"Captain Reed!" the tall, blond woman exclaimed. "You never told me how beautiful your sister is! It is a wonder she is not yet married!"

"Barronsgate's society is somewhat limited, I am afraid," replied Edmond, smiling gallantly. "No one there that would suit my sister. But I am sure you will help me find her a husband in Brighton."

"I assure you, I do not need –" began Marianne.

"Oh, I am sure she has had many proposals – such a handsome girl as she is. She must be holding out for a baronet, or a rich, old widower at least!" Mrs O'Donnel laughed. Marianne blushed, angry and ashamed.

The party filed into their box, and Marianne was thankful that she was exempt from such conversation for the duration of the performance. She was soon transfixed by the music and the actors, the costumes and the sets. It had been many years since she had been able to enjoy the lively entertainments that England's cities could offer. With tears in her eyes, she remembered the last time that her father had taken her to the opera in London. The evening's entertainment, however, ended all too soon, and she was once again forced to converse with her brother's friends while they waited for their carriages to arrive.

"I think this was a perfectly dull way to spend an evening, wouldn't you agree, Miss Reed?" asked Mrs O'Donnel with a coy smile.

"No, indeed, I rather enjoyed the performance," Marianne replied frankly.

"I suppose you have seen little of the truly delightful entertainments that London and Paris have to offer. The ballrooms, and the gardens, and such. I simply love Vauxhall!"

"It has been over a year since I have been to London," Marianne admitted, "and I have never been abroad."

"Oh, you poor dear!" cooed Mrs O'Donnel. "We must remedy that, mustn't we, Captain Reed?"

"Yes, I think we must," smiled Edmond.

"Well," Marianne said to Colonel O'Donnel with an attempt at good humour, "it would appear that you and I are at the mercy of my brother and your wife. Must we submit, do you think?"

"I'm afraid we must," O'Donnel replied, bland and faintly disinterested. "They are not a pair to be crossed. Let them have their way, Miss Reed, and the less fuss about it, the better."

"There you have it," cried his wife triumphantly. "I have assumed command of our little regiment, and my first order is that Miss Marianne Reed must allow me to acquaint her with Brighton tomorrow. Do you accept, Miss Reed?"

Marianne nodded her assent, and the arrival of their carriage just then put an end to the interview. She and Edmond climbed aboard, and as they drove away, Mrs O'Donnel waved goodnight to them enthusiastically.

"Amusing lady, is she not?" Edmond asked.

"Mm," Marianne replied, smiling for his benefit.

"You and she will become great friends, I think."

Rather than disagree, Marianne looked out the window, feigning fatigue, and watched as Brighton's streets rolled by her, taking her to the place that would very soon become her home.

The following morning, Marianne breakfasted alone once again, then settled herself into the sitting room to write to Louisa while she awaited Mrs O'Donnel's arrival.

> *I wish you were here, Louisa. I am sure that I would enjoy Brighton much more in your company. My brother is as amusing, and impulsive, and thoughtless as ever. I am sure you and I would amuse ourselves greatly, perhaps even at his expense.*
>
> *As for his friends the O'Donnels, it may perhaps be too soon to judge, but I must confess I do not like them.*

Here, she was distracted from her epistle by the sound of a carriage outside of the window. She rose, expecting Mrs O'Donnel, but was not wholly disappointed to find that the visitors were to see Edmond's neighbours, and not Marianne. Smiling, she sat back down and finished her letter home.

Pray, kiss dear little James for me, and give my regards to your husband, she wrote, and suddenly felt a pang of homesickness. She rose again, and paced back and forth before the fire.

"You certainly do rise early," came a sleepy voice from the doorway.

105

Marianne turned and smiled. "Good morning Edmond. Shall I ring for breakfast?"

"Please," he said, sitting by the window. "Will you take some chocolate with me?"

"I've already eaten," she replied, "but yes, I think I will take a cup of chocolate." They walked together to the dining room and sat down. Edmond looked at his sister for a long moment.

"I must admit," he said, "it's awfully nice to have someone to take breakfast with me."

"Then you should marry," replied Marianne lightly.

Edmond laughed. "I have no desire for a family. But I will be very happy when you come to live with me. I do get lonely sometimes." He was quiet for a long moment. "But don't you want to marry?"

"Perhaps," said Marianne in an offhand manner. "But I've met with no one who could tempt me." She could not help but blush as she spoke, and feel that she was caught in a lie.

"How about Weston?" Edmond asked. He looked closely at her and chuckled. "I see you are blushing, Mary dear. Did you get to know him well?"

"Tolerably well," Marianne replied, attempting to laugh through her discomfort. "But I'm afraid I got to know Mrs Weston much better."

"Mrs Weston!" Edmond cried with surprise. "Is Weston married?"

"Yes, he is, and they have a young son."

"Well," said Edmond, "I must confess I am surprised. He seemed such a harsh, unapproachable fellow. Never very popular with the ladies, though I imagine they found him handsome enough. What kind of woman is she?"

"A kind one, very childlike herself. I like her very much."

Edmond leaned back and smiled. "And is he very happy, do you think?"

Marianne smiled in turn. "I'm afraid he can sometimes be a rather disagreeable man, but yes, I suppose he is happy with his choice." As she said this, however, unwelcome memories nudged themselves into her thoughts, and she doubted whether what she told her brother was the absolute truth.

"And so you have been living with the Westons at Barronsgate," continued Edmond, unaware of the darkening of his sister's mood.

"Yes," she said, and paused for a moment. "Edmond...."

"Mm?" he said, taking a swallow of coffee.

"Edmond, why – how could you sell Barronsgate?" she burst out, her eyes filling with tears. "And how could you not tell me?"

He put down his breakfast and leaned forward. "I am sorry I didn't tell you, Mary. But you must know that I do not want to live at Barronsgate – I never have. Life in the country bores me. I could never live quietly as father did."

"And you find Brighton so much more amusing?" asked Marianne, a bitter, challenging note creeping into her voice.

"A trifle less dull, yes. But I do not intend to stay here forever."

"Only until your creditors will not be put off any longer, I suppose."

Edmond sighed. "No, and I am ashamed of myself, for the debts that I allowed myself to gather. But I was a foolish young man, bent on amusement. I believe that Weston meant to injure me by paying off my debts and demanding that I sell him Barronsgate. We did not part friends."

"Because of a woman?" Marianne asked, looking at him shrewdly.

Edmond smiled wryly and without humour. "Something of the sort. But I think he would be sorely disappointed to know what a favour he has done me. I do have quite a fortune left over from the sale, and I intend to use it to purchase myself some property in the colonies."

Marianne stared at him in shock. "You mean to leave England forever?"

"I do. I understand that life in the Canadas can be rather exciting. I believe that would suit me quite well."

"And what am I to do?" Marianne asked bitterly. "Follow you there and fight off the savages myself?"

Edmond laughed. "No, indeed, I do not think that life in the Canadas would suit you at all. I have already told you, I intend to find you a husband here in Brighton before I go." He took a bite of his breakfast and surveyed her for a moment. "And as for fighting off savages, I assure you, I had much rather make friends of them. Especially since they can often be one's only near neighbours in the colonies. And I've found that they can be a rather interesting people. It is a pity you won't meet any of them. I imagine that you would fine them quite as warm and friendly as I do."

"Edmond," said Marianne, refusing to allow him to derail her, "I do not want to find a husband in Brighton. I do not want to marry a rich man and keep house for him. It has been a long time since I have seen you, but you must know me well enough...." She stopped, and willed herself not to cry.

Edmond sighed. "I don't know what you want, Mary. I cannot give you back Barronsgate. I can only introduce you to a society where you might find someone who can give you another home. But if that isn't what you want, then I'm afraid you'll have to make your own fortunes." He rose and strode to the door, then stopped. "I have some errands," he said. "Will you come with me? We will see about purchasing some new dresses for you."

"No, thank you," she replied haughtily, rising also. "I have plans of my own today."

Edmond nodded, and left the room. Soon he was gone from the house also, and Marianne was once again left alone to repeat their conversation over and over in her mind, and to await the arrival of a woman whose company gave her no pleasure.

TEN

Mrs O'Donnel did not keep her promise that day, nor did she arrive on the next. Marianne was not sorry; she had taken an instinctive dislike to the woman – an impression she could not shake. Marianne spent her days in a quiet sort of solitude, walking along Brighton's waterfront with Sarah, writing letters to Louisa, visiting a local bookseller, and enjoying her purchases by Edmond's fire. Marianne began to think that she might spend the rest of her visit without hearing any more about Colonel and Mrs O'Donnel. A week after her first meeting with that couple, however, Edmond actually rose before his sister, and paid a morning visit to his friends. Marianne was just finishing her breakfast when he arrived at home to deliver some news of the Colonel and his wife.

"There's to be a public ball tonight, Mary," he said cheerfully, sitting down, and helping himself to a portion of her meal. "How long has it been since you've danced?"

"A long time, I confess," she replied, smiling.

"Mrs O'Donnel asked specifically that you be there. She said she should like to know you better."

"Oh?" *Then why did she not keep her promise and visit me?*

"It should be amusing, at any rate. And I've invited them to dine with us tonight."

"Oh," said Marianne, her smile freezing. "Oh, won't that be lovely."

"My dear Miss Reed, what a lovely gown! It is the same one you wore the other evening, is it not?" asked Mrs O'Donnel, waving for another glass of wine.

"Yes, thank you. It is." Marianne smiled, digging her nails into her palm.

109

"The colour suits you very well. But did you not bring any other gowns with you?"

"I did not expect to be much in society," replied Marianne truthfully – despite her assurances to Louisa, she had not expected to find much pleasure at all in Brighton.

Mrs O'Donnel surveyed her broadly. "I believe you are my size. Perhaps I can lend you a dress for the ball this evening."

"No, thank you," she said quickly, glancing at the other lady's plunging neckline, and the bright, almost gaudy print of the cloth. "I believe we will be late for the ball if we must stop at your home first."

"Well, then, you must allow me to take you to see the shops tomorrow afternoon."

"With pleasure." Marianne smiled graciously, remembering Mrs O'Donnel's last promise to her.

"Leave the girl alone, Esther," the Colonel interrupted, raising a thin eyebrow in Marianne's direction. "Not everyone has the same affection for baubles that you do."

Marianne could not help but blush for the Colonel's wife. She tried in vain to find something to say to fill the awkward void that followed his statement; fortunately, it was Edmond who came to the ladies' rescue.

"I believe, Mrs O'Donnel," he said grandly, raising his glass in her direction, "that a lovely woman is only improved by finery, and as handsome as my sister is, she will be very fortunate to benefit by your elegant tastes."

"Your brother is very gallant, Miss Reed," said Mrs O'Donnel conspiratorially. Then suddenly, her eyes lit up, and she grasped Marianne's hand, almost knocking over both of their glasses as she did so. "But may I not call you Marianne? You must call me Esther – I am sure we shall be great friends!"

"Oh, yes," Marianne lied uneasily. "Yes – Esther. Yes. Great friends, I am sure."

The company arrived at the ball in the Reeds' carriage that evening; they were announced, and pressed themselves into the fray of the evening's festivities. Edmond and the Colonel were soon met by other members of the regiment, and Marianne was introduced to several fresh-faced, red-coated young men whose names she could not recall, and whom she could not distinguish from one another. She soon found herself engaged for the next several dances. She allowed herself to be led about on the dance floor with a great deal of confusion, and very little pleasure.

"I understand you are acquainted with Captain Weston," one young, blond officer whose name Marianne had either not heard, or had forgotten, asked her.

"Yes," she replied, trying to avoid his inept, shuffling feet. *Why do such clumsy, awkward men attempt to dance?*

"You will give him my regards." He stepped hard on her foot.

"Yes – oh, yes, most certainly," said Marianne, her eyes filling with tears of pain.

She danced she knew not how many dances, then, at long last, was finally allowed to plead exhaustion and take a seat near the back of the room. Before she had rested long, Esther O'Donnel joined her breathlessly.

"He is such a dancer, your brother!" she laughed, throwing herself into a chair.

"Does the Colonel not dance?" asked Marianne, freeing the edge of her dress from under the other lady.

"Oh, no! There he is in the corner, sharing old stories of defeating Bonaparte at Brussels," she waved at her husband, who nodded grimly in reply, and resumed his conversation with the other officers. "He is talking of that dreadful Captain Weston, no doubt."

"Indeed!" said Marianne, surprised. "Are they friends?"

"Of a sort," Esther replied, shrugging negligently. "Weston saved my husband's life, and many others, as I understand it. That is how he earned his Captaincy. I don't imagine he would have got it any other way, for he had no money and no real importance. Indeed, he would be of no consequence at all had he not been lucky enough to be in the militia at such a time."

The colour rose to Marianne's cheeks as she remembered Weston's bitter confessions to herself. His words rang suddenly in her ears – *I earned my Captaincy at Waterloo, I have gained the respect of those that you call the better families.* Suddenly, she wanted to slap this woman for speaking of him so, to reach out and strike her rouged face, and stop the words from her mouth. Instead, she smiled and murmured some unintelligible reply.

"It is a pity that your brother was not enlisted then," continued Mrs O'Donnel, oblivious to her listener's mood, "or else he would have my husband's rank, at least."

"I don't believe that he intends to remain in the military," Marianne replied, clutching the edge of her skirt in her fist. "He spoke of making a home for himself in the Canadas."

"The Canadas!" exclaimed the Colonel's wife, her smile suddenly gone. "Oh, but he mustn't! That is –" she said, regaining her composure, "he is such a man of fashion, I am sure he cannot mean to remove himself from good society entirely. No, indeed, it would be too bad. My husband would miss him sorely."

"Perhaps not," said Marianne, surveying her new friend with a cold shrewdness. "Though I cannot think of anything that might tempt him to stay."

"Oh, I suppose not," said Mrs O'Donnel with a shrill, silvery laugh. "If his feelings were engaged, it would be different, I imagine."

Edmond himself saved his sister from further comment by finding his way to them with a gracious bow and smile. "It is a shame to see two such lovely ladies in want of a partner. I am afraid it would not do to ask you to dance, Mary, but perhaps Mrs O'Donnel will allow me to rescue her."

"Edmond," Marianne interrupted. "I'm afraid the noise and the exercise have given me a headache. Will you send for the carriage? I will have Paul return for you after I arrive home."

"Of course," Edmond replied with an apologetic smile to Mrs O'Donnel. He offered his arm to his sister, and led her across the room. "Are you ill, Mary?"

"No, only tired," she replied with a smile. *And I have much to think about.* She nodded a polite goodnight to Mrs O'Donnel, who resettled into her chair with ill-disguised ill-humour. Then she allowed Edmond to lead her through the hot, crowded room, through the music and laughter, and the crush of rich and stylish and fashionable people.

When at last they were outside, she exhaled slowly, smiling faintly at Edmond's offhand, yet boyishly concerned postulations about her health. And before long, Marianne was in the carriage, rolling along the dark, quiet streets, then she was at home, allowing Sarah to unbind her hair, and finally, she was in bed, lying wide awake and staring at the blank ceiling above her. She couldn't help but be unhappy when she reflected on what Edmond's and Esther's relationship might be. She could not imagine that he would endanger his career or his own reputation by dallying seriously with a married woman; however, he was irresponsible enough to allow himself to be entangled. And even if Esther were not married, Marianne felt that she could not be pleased by any sort of relationship that she and Edmond might have. Marianne sighed and forced herself to think of other things. What was it that Esther had said of Captain Weston? He had saved several lives at Waterloo. Despite herself, Marianne smiled. She could not help but be pleased by this testimony of her friend's bravery. She allowed her thoughts to take the more pleasant turn that her recollections of Esther O'Donnel's account of Weston brought about. And before long, Marianne was peacefully asleep, lost in an impossible dream about Barronsgate and Captain Weston.

The following morning, Marianne was awakened by Sarah, who threw open the curtains to reveal the bright day outside.

"Is it not very early yet?" Marianne murmured sleepily, blinking at the light.

"It is after nine, Miss," replied Sarah, tying back the curtains. "Mrs O'Donnel is arrived to see you."

"Already?" asked Marianne, sitting up.

"Yes, Miss. She is in the drawing room with Captain Reed."

"Help me with my dress, then," Marianne said, staring regretfully at her bed. "I suppose I must not keep her waiting long."

"Marianne! How well you look this morning," cried the Colonel's wife, as Marianne stepped through the doorway into the stuffy, seldom-used drawing room. Esther rose and embraced her showily, then resumed her seat upon the sofa.

"Thank you. You have not been waiting long, I hope," Marianne

113

said, sitting down and accepting some bread and preserves from the silent, sullen Collins. "Will you have some breakfast?"

"No – no thank you, I've already eaten. And yes, I've waited for you an age, at least. But your brother has been keeping me company."

"Good morning, Edmond," said Marianne, turning towards her brother, who stood a little apart, by the hearth. "Did you stay very long last night?"

"Not long," replied Edmond, stirring the fire absently.

"It was very dull after you left, Marianne," cooed the Colonel's wife. "How very cruel of you to leave us, my dear."

Marianne smiled and said nothing. *How insincere she is!*

"Do hurry with your breakfast, Marianne," said Edmond, turning away from the fire.

"Yes, do!" Esther O'Donnel cried. "I must show you the best shops and warehouses. We will make you a lady of fashion, I think. You will be quite the sensation in the spring – I will make you my protégée, and then we will see how many suitors you will have!"

"Thank you," Marianne managed to murmur, and she bit her lip to keep from saying more. She hastily finished her breakfast, then followed Mrs O'Donnel into the hall.

"We must get you a new cloak," said Marianne's kind protector, fingering the garment critically. "This one is frightfully out of fashion!"

"Thank you," Marianne said again, almost fleeing out the door. Esther followed close on her heels, chattering about colours and sleeves, feathers and India shawls. Marianne's head began to spin as they flew from shop to shop, and Esther exclaimed over the various styles and fabrics. Dresses and cloaks, bonnets and slippers and other trifles swam before her until she could hardly tell which ones she truly liked, and which ones Mrs O'Donnel insisted that she must like.

"No, no – I am quite sure that I do not need four ball gowns," Marianne protested in one shop, and in another, "It may be plain, but it is very practical – and who of consequence will see me in my riding dress?" Occasionally, she managed to prevail over her kind friend, but at the end of the day, she had purchased so many hats, gowns, gloves and slippers, she could hardly tell whether she herself had actually chosen any of them. Her ears were fairly ringing with Esther's cries and exclamations as they walked home, having entrusted the various packages to Sarah's and Paul's care.

"Tell me, Marianne," whispered Esther conspiratorially, "have you no one you wish to impress in your new finery?"

An image of Captain Weston came unbidden to Marianne's mind. She shook her head and replied firmly, "No, none."

Esther laughed. "You blush! I think you lie!"

Marianne walked on in determined silence.

"Come now – haven't you a lover?"

Marianne stopped. "No, indeed," she replied haughtily. Her indignation rose, and yet an uncomfortable feeling that she was lying washed over her.

"More the pity," replied Esther, walking on ahead. "Husbands are necessary, of course, but they are nothing to a young man very much in love – they can be so ... ardent."

Heat rushed again to Marianne's cheeks as she surveyed her companion with disdain. "For my part, I had rather the love and admiration of a husband."

Esther laughed. "Yes, perhaps, but who can marry for love anymore? For *my* part, I will have my lovers, and my husband will have his." All at once, she stopped and clapped her hands with glee. "Oh, but that's it!"

"What?" replied Marianne irritably.

"It is you – and he! You wish to be my husband's lover! It is him that you wish to impress! He is old, but I think he is still handsome – don't you?"

Marianne's stomach turned at the thought of the surly, portly Colonel. "You are mistaken, I assure you," she said hotly.

"My dear Marianne, do not imagine I am jealous! You may have his affections if you want them. In fact, I have a lover of my own!"

"Really."

"Yes, and shall I tell you who it is?" Mrs O'Donnel teased, walking on ahead. Marianne would not take the bait, so Esther turned and replied, "It is Edmond – your brother! Are you not surprised?"

They arrived just then in front of Edmond's home; Marianne stopped and surveyed the blond woman coldly. "I thank you for your company today. Give my regards to the Colonel." And with that, she spun on her heel, stalked up the stairs, and snapped shut the door of the house behind her without once looking back.

"Mary?" Edmond called from the sitting room. "Is Mrs O'Donnel with you?"

"No," Marianne said, placing her cheek on the cool wall that separated them. "No, I am alone." She breathed in deeply, trying to calm herself.

"Has she not the finest taste? Did I not tell you she is a lady of fashion?"

"Yes."

"Did you buy a great many things today?"

"Yes," she said again, without moving.

"Mary? Why do you not come and sit with me? Collins has just brought in the tea things. I do not much like eating alone."

"No." Marianne cleared her throat and straightened herself before she stepped forward into the doorway to face him. "No, thank you. I have a headache."

"Again?" Edmond looked up with concern. "Are you ill?"

"No," said Marianne tilting her chin defiantly. "I believe it is Mrs O'Donnel's incessant, inane chatter. It makes my head ache – I do not believe I have heard her speak two words of sense. She is such a silly, insincere creature!"

Edmond looked up, surprised. "You are very harsh – I hope that she does not speak so ill of you."

"And I hope she does," Marianne replied hotly. "I do not want the praise or the esteem of such a woman. Really, she has no sense, no principles. I have no doubt that a woman like that would have no scruples about breaking her marriage vows, if her own pleasure was at stake. I don't believe that I want you to associate with such a common, unprincipled woman, Edmond."

Edmond could only stare at his sister in wonder. "I am going up to my room, Edmond," said she. "Have Sarah bring me my tea there." And she stalked up the stairs in silence, wanting to smash her fists upon every wall as she went. *Horrid, selfish man!* she thought.

How could he entangle himself with such a creature?

She shut herself into her room, trying to contain her shame and her frustration; Sarah knocked timidly on the door and brought in the tea, but Marianne found that she could not eat. She stared at the packages in the corner of the room, and fought the impulse to burn them all, or to throw them through the window and dash them upon the street below. Finally, she stepped carefully over to the many paper-wrapped bundles, and searched until she found what she was looking for – a small one that she had herself chosen while Esther was occupied with the purchase of a bonnet for herself. Hugging the little package to her chest, Marianne crept down the stairs and to the sitting room. Edmond was not there. Marianne placed the package on the chair next to the fire and went out to find Collins.

"He's gone, Miss," that servant told her blandly.

"Has he gone to see the O'Donnels?" Marianne asked quietly.

"I believe he has, Miss."

Marianne sighed. "Thank you, Collins." She returned to the sitting room to write another letter to Louisa, but very soon found that she could find nothing to say. *I wish that you were here*, she wanted to write, *so that I could speak to you, seek your advice.* Instead, she wrote nothing, and simply stared out of the darkened window. Finally, when her shoulders tightened painfully and her hand cramped from holding the pen in her hand, she returned to her bedroom, to surrender herself to a restless, fitful night's sleep.

ELEVEN

Merry Christmas, Edmond," said Marianne, as she joined her brother for a late breakfast.

"That's not until tomorrow," he replied, barely looking up.

"Yes, I know. But I think I will return home tomorrow."

He looked up, surprised. "I thought you were to stay another week, at least!"

"I am sorry. But I do miss Barronsgate, and it won't be long before I cannot return home. And I miss Louisa dreadfully."

"Louisa? Louisa Weston?" said Edmond, and Marianne was almost certain that his face blanched. *Good God, is he still in love with her?*

"Yes, and from her letters I can see that she misses me too. Other than Captain Weston and little James, she has very little company there." Her brother did not reply for a long moment, and his face was turned away from hers. "Edmond, did you hear me?"

Captain Reed sighed and set down his cup. "Yes, yes," he said without looking up. "If you must go … but I really had wished you would stay longer."

"I know. But before long, I will be back in Brighton, and then I will not leave," Marianne paused, and tried to appear cheery at the prospect. "But here – I have a little present for yo."

Edmond smiled as he took the small package from her, and opened it. "They're lovely, Marianne," he said, examining the cuff links inside. "Thank you."

"I was going to bring you father's," Marianne confessed, her eyes misting with tears, "but they are not very nice, I am afraid, and one is broken."

"Come," said Edmond, rising and taking his sister's hand. "I have a little present for you, too." He led her into the sitting room, and pulled open a large desk drawer. "There," he said, producing a package. "Now you must tell me that you like it, whether you do or no."

Inside, she found a warm, heavy fur-lined cloak. She held it up to herself with pleasure.

"I know that … some of the fashionable ladies of Brighton are not always very practical," he said, blushing. "I thought you might like this better than the ones you saw in the shops yesterday."

"I do," she replied honestly, embracing him. "And it is a cold day today – will you take a walk with a young lady in a very practical, unfashionable cloak?"

"I will, with pleasure," Edmond replied, smiling and offering his arm. "But not just now. Have you any plans for the afternoon?"

"None at all," replied Marianne with a smile, "except to pack my trunks."

"Be a good girl then, and let me finish my breakfast in peace," he said, resuming his place by the fire. His sister cuffed him lightly upon the head with mock indignation before she left the room. And when she turned at the bottom of the stairs, she saw that he was not eating at all, but was only staring into the gentle flames of the dying fire.

That afternoon they walked out along the water's edge, Marianne wrapped warmly in her new cloak, and Edmond strolling complacently at her side. Carriages rolled by, and they passed several people along the way – merchants and fishmongers, children at play, and fashionable people as well, and it struck Marianne that she no longer found the place as noisy and jarring as she once had, not so many days ago. *But it is nothing to country life*, she thought sadly, thinking of the quiet and solitary walks that she had grown up loving on and about the grounds at Barronsgate. She shook herself. *No, I must no longer think so. Before long, this is to be my home.* She smiled at Edmond, who had been silent for a long while. "What are your thoughts?" she asked.

"Oh," he said offhandedly, "I am afraid there is very little on my mind. I will miss you while you are away." he paused and walked on a little further. "Tell me about the Westons. Tell me about … Mrs

Louisa Weston. That is her name, is it not?"

"It is," Marianne replied. She wondered what to tell her brother – she did not want to cause him any pain. She decided not to tell him that she knew that he and Louisa had been acquainted before her marriage to Weston. "She is a very sweet, impulsive lady, and sometimes very childlike – sometimes, she seems hardly more than a girl. I confess that her moods are very changeable, and she can be very timid, but where she loves, she loves a great deal." Marianne stopped, and thought suddenly of Esther O'Donnel. "And she is very devoted to the Captain, and to her son."

"And the son's name is James?"

"Yes. A very good child, I think, though I have very little experience with children."

"And is he very like his mother?" Edmond asked, not looking at his sister.

"Yes," said Marianne, though her heart ached for her brother. "I suppose he is, but he is so young – he may turn out more like his father." *And I believe that you, Edmond, wish that you were his father!*

"And Weston – he takes good care of them?"

"The best of care. I believe that he loves them very much."

Edmond laughed, but it was a short, brittle sound to Marianne's ears. "I never thought he would marry – I suppose that it is best that he should have someone that he can take care of."

"Yes," said Marianne, her own heart suddenly contracting in her chest. And they walked on in silence for some time before they were able to chatter about things of little consequence. They returned to the little house that they were soon to share, and spent the remainder of the afternoon by a warm fire. They dined together that evening, and retired early to bed, brother and sister suddenly very much depressed by the parting that must follow in the morning.

Marianne slept well that night, and rose early to pack her trunks. She looked long at the new packages that were to return to Barronsgate with her, before finally resolving herself to put on her new travelling costume. *After all, they are mine. There is no reason I should not wear them!* She dressed, and could not help but admire her reflection in the mirror. *I should think that I would not be so much out of place here in Brighton, now.*

She went down, and was pleased to find her brother already in the dining room.

"You have become such an early riser!" she teased, sitting opposite him.

"It is my sister," he replied with mock-seriousness. "She had quite the sobering effect on me. I declare, if she stays much longer, I will be taking orders."

"Oh, indeed!" Marianne laughed. "You would make a fine minister, if only you would rise early enough to make sermons. I suspect you are only up now to see your sister safely away, and be sure she will plague you no more."

"You are quite right," said Edmond, "and also to be sure she will not stay away for long. I rather like the steadying influence she has on me. And perhaps she will bring home some similarly steady young lady friends, that I might find myself a wife."

Marianne smiled. "I would gladly find you a wife if only she would convince you to stay in England." She thought suddenly of Esther O'Donnel, and wondered whether it was best to encourage Edmond to stay, or to hurry him away. "You will write to me, will you not?"

Edmond smiled ruefully. "I will promise to write, if it will make you happy. But it might make a liar of me, for you know I am no great correspondent."

"Yes," said Marianne, "I know." She paused a long moment. "Edmond, I am very happy that we could … reacquaint ourselves. And I will miss you."

"Of course you will. Who would not miss such a handsome and dashing and wildly amusing man as me?"

Marianne laughed. "Who indeed?"

Sarah appeared at in the doorway then. "The carriage is ready, Miss."

"Well," said Marianne, rising. "You are rid of your house guest, sir."

"Come back soon, Mary."

"I will," she replied, embracing her brother. She looked at him then; she knew she would miss him, but at that moment, she could not help but wish that she were embracing someone else. She pulled away, and moved towards the door.

Edmond waved at the carriage as it rolled away. Marianne sat back against the seat and closed her eyes, wanting to sleep away the hours that would lead her back to Barronsgate.

Somehow, the journey home to Barronsgate seemed much longer than the trip to Brighton. But at last its familiar, warm brick walls appeared past the well-known and beloved trees and hills, and it was all Marianne could do not to leap from the carriage and run down the lane.

She had written home to tell Louisa that she would be returning sooner than she had first expected, but she had never specified what day she would arrive. She therefore had the joy of surprising her dear friend, who first appeared at the sitting room window, then burst through the front door to greet the road-weary traveller.

"Marianne!" the petite woman cried, opening the carriage door before it had fully stopped. A brown and white terrier followed her out of the house, barking excitedly at the horses. "You are home! Was Brighton so unpleasant? Did you and Captain Reed not get on well?"

"Not at all," replied Marianne, allowing herself to be warmly and childishly embraced. "I was very glad to see Edmond. But I missed you, my dear, and Barronsgate." *And the Captain as well.* "And Brighton will be my home soon enough. I cannot say the same of Barronsgate. Do you think Jason has missed me?" she asked, offering the little dog her gloved hand to sniff.

"Oh, no, don't!" cried Louisa, ignoring her friend's question. "Don't talk of leaving again when you have only just arrived!"

"Very well," Marianne laughed, scooping Jason up into her arms and letting him lick her face excitedly. "Then let us talk of the presents I have brought you."

"You need not have brought presents," Louisa admonished, leading her friend inside. "We are happy you are returned – that is present enough."

"I hope James will like them then, if you won't," said Marianne, handing the dog to Louisa, who put him back outside, and taking off her cloak.

"Oh, Marianne, you are so fashionable!" Louisa turned her friend by the shoulders, admiring her new dress. "Surely you were the loveliest young lady in Brighton!"

"Without a doubt," said Marianne with mock-seriousness. "Now come – I am very cold. Let us warm ourselves by the fire, and you and James will open your presents. And...." Marianne paused, then forced a light smile before she continued. "where is Captain Weston? Have I chased him away?"

"No, indeed," said Louisa, leading the way to the cosy sitting room. "I am sure he has missed you almost as much as I have. He has been quiet and restless since you've been away. He rides out alone every day, then returns home and shuts himself up alone in the library."

Marianne forced a laugh. "He has missed arguing with me! What a disagreeable, confrontational man."

"No – what a kind-hearted, affectionate man. You must believe me, for who knows him better than his – than I?"

"Who, indeed?" said Marianne quietly. Her heart fell as she supplied the word *wife* to Louisa's sentence. "Come now," she said, leaning forward. "Have Mrs Frawley bring down James, and send Sarah for your presents."

Marianne and Louisa settled themselves comfortably in the warm, familiar room, and James was brought down, and shyly clung to his mother's neck as he surveyed Marianne.

"What!" Marianne coaxed him gently. "Am I a stranger? I shall be very sad indeed if you will not greet me!" But little James persisted in his shyness until Sarah brought in the packages. "This is for you – a Christmas gift from this frightening stranger!"

The paper and ribbons proved too much for the young gentleman's shyness. He was soon lured from his mother's lap to tear into the packages, and before long, was settled comfortably on the carpet, where he played happily with his new Christmas toys.

"Aren't these exquisite!" cried Louisa as she examined the finely crafted little soldiers, which James soon managed to pry from his mother's hands.

"You mustn't play with them, Louisa dear," teased Marianne.

"You see, they are not for you. You will have to be content with your own presents!"

"Oh Marianne, you have not brought presents for me!" Louisa protested, blushing.

"Indeed I have!" said Marianne, handing her friend a large, bulky package.

"Oh, you mustn't! Oh, how kind!" Louisa cried, her eyes lighting up as she tore into the packages. "Oh! It is lovely!"

"See, now you must learn to become a proper horsewoman," said Marianne, smiling as she enjoyed her friend's pleasure, "for I have had a riding costume made up for you in the latest Brighton fashions! We will have Sarah fit it properly for you tomorrow."

"Oh, thank you, Marianne!" Louisa breathed, fingering the material. "But you shall have to wait until Philip comes home until we will allow you to open your Christmas presents, for it is he who picked them out!"

"Indeed?" asked Marianne, masking her surprise and emotion by playing with little James, who was enthralled by his own Christmas gifts. "Did he find them in the village?"

"No – he went to London while you were away."

"Did he! And you did not go with him?" Marianne asked, keeping her eyes on the boy rather than on his mother.

"Marianne – you know how little I like London," Louisa replied, setting her new dress carefully aside. "And I must confess, he was in rather a black mood before he left. I am afraid that I was a little glad to be rid of him."

"Louisa!" laughed Marianne in surprise, looking suddenly at her friend.

"Yes, I know, you must be shocked to hear me say such things," said Louisa, blushing.

"Only surprised that you would say them! I declare, I am having a dreadful effect on your sweet temper!"

"Oh, dear, no! Philip and I have always–" Louisa's blush deepened as she fumbled for words. "That is, we have not always gotten on as well as we do now."

"Did you know the Captain a long time before you were married?" asked Marianne, thinking suddenly of her brother.

125

"Yes – that is – yes. For a very long time."

Marianne took pity upon her friend's distress, and wondered whether she, too, were not thinking of Edmond. *What was my brother to you?* she wondered. *And what was Weston to you then, too?* For a moment, she searched her mind for something to say, some other little thing to tell Louisa, but she was prevented by the sound of footsteps in the hall.

"There is Philip!" cried Louisa, rising. "I will tell him you are home!" And she rushed happily out of the room, leaving Marianne to worry about her own composure.

Moments later, before Miss Reed was even able to calm her breathing, the Captain and Mrs Weston were in the room, and the Captain was stooping to take Marianne's hand.

"I trust your journey was a pleasant one?" he asked, releasing her fingers, and taking a chair near the fire. He was just out of the range of her vision – Marianne would have to turn her head to speak to him.

"Yes – thank you," she replied. Her voice sounded shrill to her ears. She tried to occupy her fingers with one of James's toy soldiers, which he had deposited in her lap.

"And your brother is well?"

"Oh yes, quite well. He – he sends his regards."

"Does he?" Marianne heard him shift in his chair, and fought the urge to turn and look at him. "Will you like to live with him, do you think?"

"Philip!" Louisa scolded, scooping James up into her arms and resuming her seat with the little boy in her lap. "Marianne is just returned home! Let's not think of her leaving again."

"But I must leave again, in only a few months' time," said Marianne, hoping that she sounded as cheerful as she intended. "It won't do to pretend that I will not. Yes, Captain, I believe that I will be very happy in Brighton."

"Indeed?"

"Yes – it is a very amusing place, and his friends are so very – fashionable. Edmond is very happy there, and I believe that I will be, as well." *I must not let him see my face. He will know at once what I am thinking.*

126

"I have never been much fond of fashionable people," said the Captain, and he sounded so bitter that Marianne turned and looked at him in surprise. "I find that fashion is often very far from virtue. But I am sure that you, Miss Reed, must find such society very interesting."

The colour rose quickly to Marianne's cheeks as she recalled their first meeting – had he not used those same words – *virtue* and *interesting* – then? "I believe that you are trying to imply something very vulgar, Captain," she said, her voice shaking. Her eyes were locked on to his – he allowed them to betray a cruel sort of mischief in their flinty grey depths.

"You must forgive me then. My upbringing was not carried out in the same genteel, fashionable society that you have always known. I am afraid that I am a vulgar man by nature."

"I have always believed, sir," Marianne replied, rising, "that one can overcome one's nature, if one only desires to do so. You are certainly acquainted with more genteel and virtuous people now than you were once accustomed to. As you once told me, you have made available to yourself those advantages that people like myself have long enjoyed. If you are still a vulgar man, you have only yourself to blame." She turned then to her friend, who was sitting very still in her chair. Little James was beginning to squirm and fuss in her lap, but Louisa held him firmly. Her eyes were downcast, and her cheeks had become pale and pinched. Marianne felt a twinge of pity, but she could not help but obey her instinct to leave the room as quickly as possible. She reached down and touched her friend's hand. "I am very tired, Louisa. I believe I will retire. Please have Sarah bring me my supper later." And without looking back towards Weston, she stalked out of the room and up the staircase.

Once she was safely in her own bedroom with the door closed behind her, Marianne paced angrily back and forth, her hands balled in fists, and her pale cheeks marked by angry tears. She wanted to fly at the Captain, to strike him, to pull at his hair, to cause some sort of reaction in him. *How dare he?* she raged silently. *How dare he have this effect on me with only his words, when I have none on him?* She remembered her guilt and her shame and her painful, twisted desire in the days and even weeks that followed their encounter on the hilltop, and she recalled his placid, almost indifferent avoidance of her in that time. *Why does he not feel things as I do? Why is the torment all my own?* Then, all at once, she remembered her own feelings about Edmond's involvement with Esther O'Donnel, and her brother's calm, tranquil enjoyment of that woman's company – Esther's animation when her brother turned his attentions to her, and Edmond's unruffled, self-indulgent admiration, and all at once, she knew that all of the enjoyment was on his side, and what little emotion there was in their liaison was hers. All at once, she recognised in their relationship her own acquaintance with Captain Weston! The recognition had a sobering effect on Marianne. All at once her tears stopped, and she sat down calmly upon her bed, feeling that suddenly, his influence upon her was lifted. She felt light, absolved. She wiped her tears from her cheeks and rang for Sarah. While she waited, she sat in the half-gloom of her bedroom, unmoving, unfeeling almost – she simply stared out of the window onto the darkening lawn, her hands folded in her lap, her breath shallow and quick, her mind nearly blank. At last, Sarah knocked timidly and entered her mistress's bedchamber.

"I don't intend to take my Christmas dinner alone, Sarah," she said, turning her head towards the door. "Please help me dress. And inform the Westons that I will dine with them after all."

Sarah nodded and obeyed in silence. Marianne descended at dinnertime, and was the first to take her place in the dining room. Louisa and her husband soon followed.

"You look lovely, Marianne," said Louisa, embracing the young woman. "Is that a new gown?"

"It is, thank you. You look lovely yourself. I seldom see you dressed so finely," Marianne smiled, taking her friend's hand. She felt a sudden rush of warmth towards the young Mrs Weston, as though she were being reconciled with an adversary.

"I seldom have occasion," replied Louisa, blushing as she took her seat. "The dress is a Christmas gift from Philip." She fingered the cream-coloured satin delicately, almost fearfully.

"What an attentive husband you have!" said Marianne, turning towards him. "Merry Christmas, Captain Weston." She handed him a small package – one that she had chosen when she had managed to visit the Brighton shops without Esther O'Donnel's oppressive counsel and intervention. "I was going to give you your gifts after dinner, but I wasn't able to wait on Louisa's and James's account. I suppose it would be cruel to make you wait." She said all this, looking unflinchingly into his bland, handsome face – said it so calmly that she believed she might as well be speaking to a stranger, or to the remotest acquaintance.

"Thank you," he replied, accepting the gift.

"We do have a present for you too," Louisa interrupted, "it is in your library – shall I have someone fetch it?"

"No, indeed," said Marianne, laughing. "You must know that patience is one of my many virtues."

The Captain unwrapped the package, and Louisa suddenly exclaimed with joy, "Oh, Philip! Isn't it odd!"

"Pope," said Weston, turning the book in his hand. "Thank you, Miss Reed."

Marianne felt a momentary pang as she remembered the care that she had taken in selecting that volume of poetry – Pope had long been a favourite of hers. But she smiled indifferently, mimicking Captain Weston's coolness, and was able to enjoy her Christmas dinner in a warm companionship with Louisa and in a composed civility with Louisa's husband. Dinner ended, and the Westons retired, leaving Marianne to seek out the warm fire and warmer familiarity of her father's library – now her library. Soon to become Captain Weston's library.

"Merry Christmas, Father," she murmured as she fingered the familiar old volumes upon the shelves. She turned to the desk, warm tears still upon her cheeks, and saw the package that the Captain had laid upon it. She picked it up, and pulled away the paper.

"*The Life and Opinions of Tristram Shandy, Gentleman*," she read aloud, running her finger along the cover of the first volume, beautifully bound in soft guilded leather.

"Are you familiar with Mr Sterne?" came a voice from behind her.

Marianne almost dropped the book as she spun around. "Captain! I did not hear you come in." She smiled, composing herself. "Yes –

I've read his *Sentimental Journey*. I rather enjoyed it."

"*Tristram Shandy*'s always been a favourite of mine," said the Captain. He frowned slightly as his eyes glanced over her cheeks, her eyes. Marianne remembered her tears and wiped at them furtively.

"This must be a very trying day for you," said the Captain, offering her his handkerchief. Marianne nodded curtly as she accepted it.

"Thank you. I'm doing tolerably well, I think." She hovered for a moment, unsure how to escape their *tête-à-tête*.

"I hope we shall not be enemies this winter," the Captain said at last, picking up a volume of his gift to his wife's friend.

Marianne started slightly. "No, indeed," she said, walking over to the window. "What a thought!" she laughed. The sound rang false to her ears.

"Good."

The room was silent for a moment as Marianne watched Weston's reflection in the darkened window. He was standing still, the book in his hand, gazing at its cover. All at once he laid it down on the desk as though it had burnt him. "Good night Miss Reed," he said, not looking at her. "Merry Christmas." And he strode out of the room before she could reply.

Marianne stood at the window for a long time, staring at the bright rectangle of light that the doorway of the library reflected in the shining glass. She breathed in slowly, running her hands down the front of her skirt. *He has no influence over me*, she told herself firmly as she turned, ready to go to bed, to retire at last. *We shall not be enemies – we shall be as two strangers who share a house.* And she realised that she still held his handkerchief in her hand – she had balled it into her fist, as though she wished to conceal it there.

TWELVE

Marianne and Captain Weston spent the next few weeks in a mutual silent war, filled with uneasy truces, guarded overtures and brief and brilliant battles of words and tones and half-formed accusations and implications. Marianne was often reminded of the Captain's aptitude for cruelty and vulgar implications, and equally as frequently as she was pricked by this harsher side of his nature, she was unguarded by his overtures towards conciliation and even kindness. Their existence together seemed a treacherous path – every reference to Barronsgate brought about heated references to Marianne's gentility and the Captain's humble childhood, every mention of Brighton caused her to bristle when she considered Edmond's belief that Weston's purchase of their home had arisen from malicious motives, and every mention of Edmond himself caused the Captain to lash out, Marianne believed, to injure the sister of his absent adversary. Only Louisa and James were able to bring about any sort of conciliation, as both Marianne and Weston wanted to protect both mother and child from any sort of unpleasantness.

Louisa herself could not be wholly shielded from her husband's and her friend's animosity, and attempted, in her own sweet and subtle way, to please them both by attempting to anticipate their desires. She visited the Farthingtons, and even attempted to convince Marianne to join her for her morning calls; she invited the tenants to the house for tea, she went riding with Marianne and tried to take an interest in her husband's business affairs. Marianne loved and pitied her friend for the attempts, and every morning, she promised herself that she would get along with Weston for Louisa's sake, and every evening, she retired to her room, frustrated by yet another angry or cold exchange that she and the Captain had shared that day.

All the while, her conviction that he was now powerless over her remained unwavering. *He is simply an unpleasant man with whom I must share my home a few months more.* And so she strengthened her mind to that conviction, and filled her time in her library, or helping Louisa to improve her horsewomanship, calling on her father's friends, sitting with Louisa and some of the less boorish tenants over tea, and paying morning calls in the neighbourhood with the young Mrs Weston. She even allowed her dear friend to lead her for a morning visit with Charlotte and Antonia Farthington! *At least a visit with them will be more pleasant than another confrontation with Captain Weston,* Marianne thought, though she did not wholly believe it.

"Why, Miss Reed!" cried Charlotte Farthington as she grasped Marianne's hand in her own. "How fortunate for you! I declare, the neighbourhood can be so dull. I do not know what we would do if Papa did not allow us to visit our aunt in London two or three times a year – but Brighton is such an exciting city! Will you try sea-bathing, do you think?"

"I haven't–"

"Of course, the neighbourhood will suffer without you. But it is fortunate that dear Louisa will remain at Barronsgate. I declare, I've become rather attached to our dear Mrs Weston – really, she's become indispensable to our little society."

Marianne winced as she sipped her tea, then managed to smile at Louisa, who was sitting quite mutely next to the equally mute Antonia Farthington.

"Won't you miss her terribly, dear Marianne?" Charlotte asked, nibbling on a sweetmeat.

"Indeed I will," Marianne replied truthfully, grateful for the small silence that filled the room. She turned to the other Miss Farthington.

"And when is your wedding to be?" she asked with a sympathetic smile.

"Oh – not until the summer. Mama said that we could not possibly have everything ready until June. And her relations will be coming from France – there is so much still to be done." Antonia Farthington spoke so quietly that Marianne had to lean forward to hear her, but the pretty girl's cheeks coloured with a warm blush that belied her enthusiasm.

"You must be very impatient – and Mr Christianson as well," said Marianne kindly. Antonia's blush deepened as she smiled in reply.

"And you, Marianne," Charlotte interrupted, the crumbs from her morsel still on her lips. "When are you to wed?"

Marianne attempted to laugh at the impertinence of the question. She looked to Louisa for help, but Mrs Weston seemed dumbfounded by Miss Farthington's exuberance. "Sometime after I make an acquaintance, form an attachment and accept a proposal," she replied at last.

"Oh, but I am sure that Captain Reed will introduce you to a great many rich and handsome young men! He is so handsome himself – I cannot imagine his friends will be any less so!" She turned then to Louisa, "Have you met Captain Reed, Louisa?"

"Why, I–" Louisa stammered, and looked beseechingly at Marianne, who could not think of anything to say to help her friend.

"He's very handsome, and charming. I declare!" she laughed. "If he were to return to the neighbourhood, I might marry him! He is not yet married, is he, Marianne?"

"Why, no, he–"

"You see, Antonia!" cried Charlotte, clapping her hands in delight. "I have hope yet! It is a pity you don't know him, Louisa, but I am sure you will go to visit Marianne in Brighton, and then she will introduce you."

Louisa had become slightly pale. Marianne glanced worriedly at her friend and broke in. "She might not have the chance to meet my brother. I am afraid he does not intend to stay long in Brighton. He speaks of going to the Canadas."

"Really!" Charlotte and Louisa spoke at the same time, but Miss Farthington's exclamation was so much louder that it almost drowned out the other voice.

"Yes – he intends to leave very soon," replied Marianne, wishing that she could change the topic of their conversation altogether.

"What a pity!" Charlotte Farthington replied. "I am sure he was very dashing in his red coat. And what about your husband, Louisa? Does he intend to remain a military man?"

"No," Louisa replied, her face still rather pale, and her voice trembling slightly. "He will retire this winter, I think."

"I always think it such a pity when a handsome young man leaves the service – handsome young men are always made handsomer by their regimentals. You will miss his red coat, I am sure, Louisa."

"No, indeed. I am always very afraid for him. I was sure he was going to be killed in Belgium." Louisa spoke with a frankness and openness that relieved Marianne. *Talk of her husband has made her forget my brother!*

"But you are too young – you could not have been married then!" Charlotte exclaimed.

"No – that is, I knew him." Louisa blushed again, and Marianne could not help but wonder when she had met Weston, and when she had met Edmond.

"How very romantic!" Charlotte gushed, oblivious once again to her guest's discomfort. "You have loved him since you were a child, I imagine."

Miss Farthington's words caused an unexpected pang in Marianne's breast. She looked down, afraid that her expression might betray an emotion that she herself did not understand. She heard Louisa attempt to speak and falter.

"Dear Louisa!" continued Charlotte. "You are among friends! You needn't be so modest. Is it not so, Antonia?"

"Charlotte," her sister scolded softly. "Let us speak of other things."

"Yes," Charlotte said, sounding rather disappointed. "The weather, I suppose."

Despite herself, Marianne smiled wryly at the young lady's cynicism. *Well, Charlotte Farthington and I have one thing in common! We neither of us have any use for polite conversation!*

Louisa and Marianne returned home that afternoon and joined Captain Weston for a late lunch. He had been out riding, he told them, and his horse had thrown a shoe. The event seemed to have soured his mood.

"The Farthingtons?" he snapped in reply to an inquiry by Louisa. "No, I won't call on them. I have no use for such silly, frivolous people. I've never heard anyone from that family speak any words of sense."

Marianne's indignation rose, even as she recognised that she had thought much the same thing only an hour earlier. "You speak very harshly, Captain. It was not so long ago that you sought out the acquaintance of such people as the Farthingtons. Are there no families in the neighbourhood whom you would condescend to visit now?"

"Aye. There are some very good farmers and tradesmen whose company I enjoy," the Captain replied between mouthfuls. "I'd be very happy if they were to call here."

"Oh, yes, I am sure," Marianne replied hotly. "And entertain them in the drawing room, or perhaps serve them pheasant and good port. You don't scruple to live like a rich man, but you won't condescend to become friends with other rich men. Slightly hypocritical, wouldn't you say?"

"When I meet a rich man who is worth my friendship, I will be his friend. I have paid my social dues in this neighbourhood, and I don't feel inclined to exert myself any further."

"My father was a rich man," said Marianne, her voice low and dangerous as she fixed Weston in her hot stare. "And I assure you, he was more than worth your friendship. But you have proved yourself a narrow-minded and arrogant man. I am not sure whether you would have been worth his. But I will tell you that he thought very highly of you, sir, whatever you might have thought of him."

He did not look up then, but continued eating. Louisa was silent, and there was not a sound in the room. Marianne stared at Weston for a very long moment before she set down her own fork and stalked wordlessly out and into the hall. She passed the housekeeper at the base of the stairs. "Have Paul saddle my horse, I will be riding out this afternoon," she called as she pounded up the stairs.

She dressed quickly in her riding clothes, and pulled on her warm cloak, her gift from Edmond. She walked out to the stables and accepted the horse silently from the young groom. She mounted without his help and spurred the horse into a gallop down the lane and along a steep and mucky trail. She rode hard, pushing the horse down narrow paths. As she and her mount to return to the house, tired at last, a branch snapped against her cheek, stinging her, and almost knocking her from the saddle. She cried out and touched her glove to her face. It came away, smeared with blood, and her eyes welled with tears of pain. She wiped them away impatiently, and turned the sweating, panting horse back towards home. It was a cold day, and she felt the tears freeze to her lashes and the blood to her cheek. She slowed the horse as they turned down the lane, and called for Paul as soon as the stables were in sight. He emerged, and she allowed him to help her dismount.

"Are you all right, Miss?" he asked worriedly, examining her face.

"Yes, thank you," she replied impatiently, handing him the reins, and heading back towards the house. Once through the door, she examined the cut in the hall mirror. *It will surely scar*, she reflected darkly. She pulled off her stained glove, and tossed her cloak over a chair. "Sarah!" she called. "Mrs Frawley!"

The housekeeper bustled out from the dining room. "You've cut your cheek, Miss," she said, hanging up Marianne's cloak.

"Yes, I know I've cut my cheek," Marianne replied peevishly. "It's why I called you. Would you do something about it?"

"I'll send for Mr Christianson," the implacable servant replied, heading towards the servants' quarters.

"I'm sure I don't need his care! Can't you help me yourself?"

Mrs Frawley returned and examined her mistress' face. "Aye. 'Tisn't as bad as all that, I suppose. I'll clean it for you, then we'll see if the doctor doesn't need to come."

"Very well," said Marianne. "I'll wait for you in the library."

The housekeeper bustled off again, and Marianne, suddenly very weary, opened the door to her sanctuary. "Captain Weston!" she exclaimed as she entered, surprised to find him already there.

"Marianne!" he said looking up from his book. "You've cut yourself."

"Yes, I know," she replied wearily, finding her place by the fire. "What are you doing here?"

"Forgive me. I only wanted a quiet place to read." He set down his book and approached her. "It's not very deep," he said, examining her cheek, "but I think it will bruise."

"Don't fret," said Marianne wryly. "If anyone should be so

impertinent as to ask about it, I will tell them that you struck me."

"I pray you would not," said Weston wryly, wetting his handkerchief with the liquid from a glass by his own chair. "This may hurt." And he dabbed gently at her cheek.

The alcohol did indeed sting her cheek. Marianne blinked and tried not to wince. "Will I be horribly scarred, disfigured for the rest of my days, do you think?" she asked lightly.

"I shouldn't think so," he said. "There." And he took the handkerchief away from her face, but remained kneeling by her side. Marianne felt the colour rise to her face. She touched her injured cheek gingerly. "No, leave it alone," said Weston, grasping her wrist gently. He held it for a moment in his strong, warm hand, and Marianne felt her breath catch. She rested her hand on the arm of the chair, and his own warm fingers remained a moment longer upon her wrist.

"Miss Marianne," he said quietly, in a gentle tone she had only heard from him on one or two other occasions, "I think that we must – try to be friends."

"Yes," said Marianne quickly, "for Louisa's sake."

"And for our own," Weston replied, his face near enough to hers that she need only lean forward and.... Marianne blinked hard to dispel the image. "I would like you to know that I esteem you – that is, I have the greatest respect for your character."

"Thank you, Captain Weston," said Marianne, attempting a polite smile. Her voice caught in her throat as she tried to reply with a warm cordiality.

There was then a gentle knock on the door, and Mrs Frawley entered with a basin of warm water.

The Captain rose to his feet. "Is that for Miss Reed's injury?" he asked. "It isn't necessary. I have attended to it." The housekeeper made a polite sound that indicated her disapproval, but Weston waved her away. "You needn't worry, Mrs Frawley. I have learned to care for worse injuries than a cut to the cheek. The army has taught me that much, at least." Mrs Frawley bobbed a curtsey and left them alone. The door clicked behind her and the Captain turned back to Marianne. He looked at her for a moment as though he were confused, as though she were a lady he had been speaking to at a ball, and whose name he had just forgotten. Then all at once, he clasped his hands behind his back and strode away from her, towards the door.

"I imagine that you would like to be left alone," he said. "Shall I send anything in for you? Perhaps a glass of wine – have you a headache?"

"No, thank you," she said, attempting to regain her own composure.

Weston nodded and turned to leave the room. Then suddenly, with his hand on the door handle, he turned back towards her. "Miss Reed," he began hesitantly, "I wish to assure you that I had nothing but the greatest respect for your father." He paused for a moment as though he wanted to say more, then quickly turned away again to go.

Marianne could only nod her thanks to him as she watched him quit the room. The door closed behind him, she turned her face towards the fire. She sat for a long time by the fire, turning the interview over and over in her mind.

Her solitude was interrupted a short while later by Louisa, who knocked timidly as she entered the library. "Marianne," she called softly from the door, "are you quite all right? Philip says you've hurt yourself."

"Yes – a little riding accident, nothing serious," Marianne said, straightening herself in her chair. "Come – sit with me by the fire."

Louisa took the chair opposite Marianne's, and peered at her friend's wounded cheek. "Oh dear! Does it hurt much?" she asked anxiously.

"Not at all. Your husband is a fine surgeon." Marianne smiled reassuringly, feeling as she did so that her face was indeed bruised as the Captain had predicted.

"Lord! I'm sure I will be too frightened to ride with you any more!" Louisa said, squeezing her friend's hand affectionately.

"You will not!" declared Marianne, laughing. "I won't let you – you've made such progress!"

"If you can injure yourself so – why, I feel my very life must be in danger every time I ride out."

"I was not being sensible," Marianne replied truthfully. "I'm afraid I was much too occupied by my quarrel with Captain Weston, and not with my horse, as I ought to have been."

"Yes – Marianne, I wish you would not quarrel any more," said Louisa, dropping Marianne's hand.

"I know – I will try, I promise."

"Philip says that he has pledged to be your friend and not your adversary."

"Oh!" Marianne said, smiling to cover her surprise. "Yes, we have formed a pact." *Captain – have you told your wife what passed between us?* Unexpectedly, Marianne's heart fell at this thought.

"I am glad. Marianne–" She looked up then, her face suddenly earnest. "I want you to understand – I would like for you and Philip to – to like each other. It is very important to me that you should be friends. Do you understand?"

"Yes," said Marianne, surprised by Louisa's earnestness. "Yes, of course."

"Good." Louisa smiled with relief. She rose from her chair. "Now – shall I have the tea things brought in here?"

"Only if you'll stay," Marianne replied with a smile.

"Of course." Louisa smiled again, and embraced her friend gingerly, as though she were afraid Marianne might shatter and break apart.

"Louisa," Marianne said suddenly as they waited for the teathings. "Do you like Charlotte and Antonia Farthington?"

Louisa looked up in surprise. "Why – they are very kind to me."

"But do you like them?"

Mrs Weston looked down then and, to Marianne, looked very much like a small child caught misbehaving. "No – I confess I don't."

"Then why do you still visit them?" Marianne persisted.

"I – I thought that it would please you ... and Philip, to know that I was visiting them." Louisa blinked, and looked very much like a little girl trying to be forgiven.

Marianne laughed suddenly. The sound seemed to startle Louisa. "Dear silly creature!" she cried. "I don't think that the Captain cares at all any more whether you notice such people. And I must confess that I don't like the Farthingtons at all!"

Louisa smiled shyly, then laughed a little. "I wish I had known that," she replied, "and I would not have spent so much time trying to please them."

"Please, Louisa – promise me not to notice anyone at all that you don't like!"

"Yes," Louisa smiled, "all right – I will promise that!"

The tea-things were brought in then, and Louisa and Marianne settled down for a pleasant meal. It began to snow that afternoon, and they sat by the window and laughed as they watched Jason chase the first flakes across the lawn, barking and leaping as he went. Then all at once, it struck Marianne that this was the last winter she was to spend at Barronsgate, that next year, she would be watching the snow fall upon the dirty streets of Brighton. A deep sadness settled upon her, and it was all she could do to put on a show of good humour for her friend. At length, however, her despondency overcame her. Pleading a headache, she retired to her own bedroom, and indulged herself in a few stray tears for the home that she was to lose when the newly falling snow left the familiar grounds of her home for another season.

THIRTEEN

And so, from a muted war, Marianne and the Captain settled into an uneasy truce; they were polite but distant whenever they met in the house or on the grounds, and by tacit accord, they each avoided any topic that might pique the other's temper. Louisa seemed relieved by this cease-fire, but the excess of manners and cordiality that hung between Weston and Marianne made that young lady almost wish for their bright and fiery animosity. She was forced to admit to herself that she often enjoyed their battles, that she liked seeing him frustrated and irritated.

Horrible man! she thought. *See how adversarial he's made me become!*

Around the same time, the weather turned unusually cold, making riding and walking unpalatable, and occasionally even impossible. So Marianne and the Westons found themselves in each other's company more than usual. Even Louisa's sweet temper began to chafe at their confinement and at the lack of variety in their days.

"James is horribly cranky today," she complained one morning, coming down from the nursery. "He won't stop throwing his toys about and pulling at Jason's ears and tail. I'm afraid that he's trying my patience frightfully these days."

"A pity he doesn't have any other children to play with," replied Marianne, coming away from the window. The snow was falling at an alarming rate, dashing her hopes that she and Louisa might ride out the following day. She sat down fitfully by the fire.

"Oh – I think he is still full young to think of such things," said Louisa, taking her friend's place by the window.

"True, I suppose. But other children would entertain him, I am sure. Some company might improve his temper. I am sure it would improve mine."

"Mine as well," Louisa conceded. "Should we have a dinner here perhaps?"

"I don't know who we would invite, apart from the Farthingtons and Mr Christianson, and they haven't any children to entertain little James," said Marianne, considering the flames in the hearth gloomily. "My father's friends are too old and too cautious to venture out in such weather."

"What about the Wilcoxes?" asked Louisa, brightening suddenly.

"Who?" Marianne asked, frowning. *Don't let them be one of those dull tenant families who speak of nothing but cattle and potatoes.*

"Mr Wilcox is a gentleman-farmer who lives on the other side of the village, not far from the Farthingtons. His wife is young and lively, and her sister lives with them as well. And the Wilcoxes have three children – the youngest is about James' age."

"Oh – yes, I'm sure that would be very amusing," Marianne lied, attempting a smile.

"But I suppose we must invite Charlotte and Antonia as well," Louisa ventured hesitantly.

"Yes, I suppose we must, although I don't know–" Suddenly, an impish thought came to Marianne and she smiled. "Oh, yes indeed, I am sure they will be thrilled by the prospect of a little evening party! Let's send out the invitations right away!"

And so, the following Saturday, Marianne's carriage was sent out to collect the Wilcoxes, and Mr Christianson arrived with his fiancée and her sister in the Farthingtons' own chaise.

"How very unfortunate that your parents could not come," said Marianne, greeting her guests.

"Yes – Papa is afraid that he will catch his death of cold in weather like this, and Mama is already unwell. I'm afraid they really could not venture as far as Barronsgate," replied Charlotte, surveying Marianne in her new dress. "Are we to be your only guests, then?"

"No, indeed," said Marianne cheerfully. "Some friends of the Captain's are coming as well. The Wilcoxes. They should be here very soon."

"Really! And are they very fashionable people, Captain Weston?"

Charlotte turned to the Captain, who was already engaged in quiet conversation with Mr Christianson in the opposite corner of the drawing room.

"They are not," Weston replied, turning. "But they are good people, and I like them immensely."

"Then I am sure we will find them vastly amusing, won't we, Antonia?" replied Charlotte, without even looking at her sister. "The Captain has such very good taste!"

The Captain bowed stiffly and returned to his conversation. Moments later, the Wilcoxes were announced. Marianne turned with interest towards the door. Mrs Wilcox and her sister Miss Thatcher entered first. Marianne was somewhat disappointed; they were pretty women, dressed simply, but with sensible taste. Louisa accepted the office of hostess and greeted them warmly, before introducing them to Marianne.

"I'm so glad you could come," Marianne smiled. "But where is Mr Wilcox?"

"Oh – my husband is outside, talking to Paul, your coachman. Paul's brother is a dear friend of ours." Mrs Wilcox was the taller of the two women, and spoke with a simple country accent. Marianne smiled to herself. *Perhaps this dinner won't be such a failure after all.*

"Wonderful," Marianne replied. "Have you met Miss Farthington, or her sister Miss Antonia?"

Soon, dinner was announced, and the company found their way to the dining room. Marianne contrived to seat Charlotte Farthington next to Mrs Wilcox, and Antonia, next to Miss Thatcher. She herself sat between Mr Christianson and Louisa. The Captain sat opposite Marianne.

"Mrs Wilcox," she asked with a gracious smile. "It was very good of you to bring your children to amuse little James in the nursery this evening. I understand they are still very young. I hope they are not too difficult to manage."

"Oh – no." Mrs Wilcox replied easily. "I have a girl from town to keep after them. She is very good."

"A governess!" Charlotte Farthington exclaimed, clearly

surprised. "How lovely for you."

"She's not a governess, really," said Mrs Wilcox. "I myself take charge of the children's education."

"I see." Charlotte smiled conspiratorially at Marianne, who managed a tight smile in response.

"I understand you are to be married soon, Miss Antonia," Mrs Thatcher said to her neighbour, who had been almost mute during the meal.

"Yes," the younger Miss Farthington replied in an almost-whisper, blushing deeply.

"And you, Miss Farthington?" Miss Thatcher asked innocently. "Are you betrothed as well?"

Marianne perceived a deepening colour that crept up from the neckline of Charlotte's gown. "No," Charlotte replied, smiling icily. "Antonia's will be the only wedding that our family can expect this year." Marianne could almost have applauded the ignorant, guileless Miss Thatcher.

The meal continued in silence for some time, until Weston and Mr Christianson led the company in an exchange of pleasantries and mundane comment about the weather. Marianne perceived that Louisa and Mr Wilcox said little, and that the two Misses Farthington were positively silent. Marianne herself conversed gaily with her guests; she could not ever recall being in company with a silent Charlotte Farthington.

Soon, after the last dish had been served, the ladies retired to the drawing room, leaving the gentlemen to smoke in the dining room. A cheerful fire had been lit, and the company broke into two groups. Louisa and Mrs Wilcox found a place by the fire, where they conversed companionably, while the Misses Farthington, Marianne and Miss Thatcher sat around a small walnut table.

"Tell me, Miss Thatcher," said Charlotte Farthington, a glint of malice in her eye, "are we to expect your wedding very soon?"

"Oh, not soon, I'm afraid," said Miss Thatcher cheerfully. Charlotte smiled triumphantly. "I won't be married until next year," continued Miss Thatcher. Charlotte's smile faded, and her expression took up a decidedly sour expression. Miss Thatcher did not seem to notice. "Joseph Pinckett – that is who I am to marry – takes over his father's millinery shop next autumn. That is when we are to marry." She beamed happily then at Marianne, who returned a warm smile.

"Indeed?" asked Charlotte with mock interest. "Your husband will make hats, will he?" She tried to share her humour with her sister, who was decidedly flustered by the exchange, and with Marianne, who was decidedly unsympathetic. Charlotte leaned back then in an unshared triumph and snobbishness.

"Yes – it is a very successful shop. And I'm so glad he's not a farmer! My father is a farmer, and they must work so very hard." Thankfully, little Miss Thatcher remained completely unaware of her new acquaintance's malice.

Marianne looked up then, and noticed that Louisa and Mrs Wilcox were silent; indeed, they were listening to the conversation in the other part of the room. Louisa's eyes met Marianne's, and Miss Reed suddenly felt ashamed. She looked down quickly.

"Oh, yes," Charlotte Farthington continued. "We will be sure to bring all of our business there, won't we, Antonia?"

Antonia murmured an unintelligible reply, and the company once again fell into a silence, made bearable only by the false sense of comfort and companionship produced by the merry crackling of the logs in the fire.

It was thus that the men found them when they at last made their way into the drawing room. A card game was suggested, and two tables were quickly set up. Marianne herself begged to be excused. Louisa was at one table, and the Captain, at the other. Marianne suddenly felt deeply ashamed of herself, and found that she was unable to meet the eyes of either Captain or Mrs Weston. So while the others played, she sat by the fire, pretending to read a book, and gazing gloomily instead into the cheerful cracking flame in the hearth.

Finally, the carriages were called, and the company left. Mr and Mrs Weston saw them all graciously off, and Mrs Weston retired to kiss her young son good night. Marianne found herself alone with the Captain.

"Well – that was a lovely evening," she said, feigning cheerful fatigue. "Very entertaining, I think."

"Really," replied Weston blandly, his back to her. "For whom?" Marianne's heart fell, but she tightened her jaw and resolved to reveal nothing of her mood. "Why, Captain!" she teased coquettishly. "Did you not enjoy yourself?"

He turned then, and there was an unusual light in his eyes. At once, Marianne felt a burst of fear and anticipation in her breast. Her breathing quickened, and her cheeks felt warm, as though she were suddenly tipsy with wine. "No, indeed, Miss Reed," he said, his voice grave, and out of keeping with the repressed animation that his features betrayed. "I assure you that Mr Wilcox and Mr Christianson and I got along famously. But I fear that the same cannot be said of the ladies."

"You men know nothing of ladies' conversation," Marianne replied lightly, wanting suddenly to tease him, to bait him, to see what emotion he was so obviously trying to hide. "I assure you, we all got on famously."

"I think you are lying, dear Miss Reed," he said, his voice low and dark. He took a small step towards her, and Marianne almost jumped. She felt as though she were wound too tightly, a spring coiled to its limit. "Tell me," he continued, leaning forward slightly, his eyes gleaming as though they emitted a cool, grey light of their own. "Who were you trying to punish? Charlotte Farthington and her sister, or Anne Wilcox and her sister? Or perhaps Louisa?"

"Captain!" Marianne laughed, and her voice rang out, clear and crisp as a wineglass, shattered upon the floor. "I am afraid you have completely misunderstood me!"

"No, I don't believe that I have," he said. Marianne perceived that they were suddenly standing very close together, and she could not remember whether it was she or he who had stepped forward. "I know you, Marianne," he said, his voice suddenly thick and uncontrolled. "I know you," he repeated, his eyes locked upon hers.

Marianne knew then that she could not stand still, could not speak, could not turn and leave. She felt electrified, held by the frightening, crackling, alluring light in his eyes. He looked at her, waiting for her, expectant and demanding. Almost without her will or her knowledge, her limbs moved towards him. Her arm reached out, her fingers pushed through his thick hair, held him there, cruelly tight, wanting to hurt him. He did not move, did not speak, and she crushed her mouth suddenly on his, kissing him so hard that she tasted blood, and still she could not release him, only kept pressing his mouth onto hers. He himself did not move, did not reach out for her, did not press her body to his, did not push her away. He accepted her kisses, but he did not move. Then suddenly, Marianne felt that she could not breathe, that she was suffocating in this embrace, and she released him, almost violently. Still, he did not move. His expression was blank, but his eyes still emanated that cold, electric grey light. He did not speak, he only stood there, cold and immobile as stone. She saw that she had cut his lip. She turned then, looking slowly at the door, and moved towards it, stumbling, as though drunk. She left him, not looking back, wanting only to find the stairs, and then her own dark bedroom. She did not look back, but she knew that he had not moved, that he was standing there, immobile, standing there, looking at her as she walked away.

Marianne closed the door of her bed chamber securely behind her, and stood in the centre of the room, breathing as though she had just run there from the end of the lane, as she used to do when she was a child – only days ago, it seemed to her suddenly. She stood still, breathing hard and staring into the fire, surrounded by the glowing gloom of the evening. She felt strangely elated, as though her body were suddenly charged with a strange lightning. And still, she felt no desire to move, indeed, she remained immobile as the glow of the fire slowly ebbed. She did not feel unearthed as she had the last time her lips had met Weston's; indeed, she felt strangely in control, almost as though, just standing there, she exerted a sort of a power over the whole of the house and all those who slept under its roof. She could no longer pretend that Captain Weston held no power over her; and yet, this understanding made her feel that she was more in control of herself than ever she had been. And she felt triumphant – she could almost laugh out loud.

At last, her body relaxed, as though she were come to life at last from a statue of stone. She rang for Sarah, and stood and waited as her maid bustled around her, uneasy and silenced by the strange light in her mistress's eyes. Her nervous fingers fumbled with the clasps on Marianne's gown, and it fell to the floor. She bent to pick it up, but Marianne stopped her.

"Leave it, Sarah," she said. "You can go now."

Sarah nodded and slipped quietly out. Marianne was once again alone. She reached up, her arms inexplicably heavy and weary, and unbound her hair, lettign it fall across her shoulders. She stepped over her dress and climbed into bed. Her cheek touched her cool pillow, she closed her eyes, and was fast and deeply asleep.

She woke late the following morning, and lay still, listening to the bustle of the household outside her bedroom door. As the morning crept to afternoon, she lay there still, unmoving, feeling strangely calm and detached from the happenings outside her bedroom. At last she rose. She rang for Sarah and dressed in silence, binding her hair in a simple knot. Then she left her bedroom, closing her door, and strode towards the servants' quarters, a sort of elastic assurance in her step. She descended the back stairs, and broke out into the cool day without passing a soul. She shivered as the frosty day settled itself upon her, then made her way to the stables. She took an old riding coat of her father's off a peg there, and wrapped herself in it. Marianne wished that she could saddle her own horse; of course, such knowledge was beyond the abilities of a lady of her station, so she was forced to seek out Paul.

He was not in the stables, so she went in search of him upon the grounds. *The world seems so still today*, she thought as she wandered across the frozen lawn, then down into the groves of trees beyond. She soon forgot the prospect of a ride as she walked out into the frosty day. The cold air brought blood to her cheeks and caused her to sniffle. Then hunger began to rumble her stomach, and she turned back and walked towards the house, her toes numb by now, and her fingers burning with the cold. Scarcely noticing, she began to hum to herself as she walked.

She entered the house through the front door, and strode into the library, where she rang immediately for her tea. Then she stood warming her hands by the fire. She heard footsteps behind her.

Without turning, she said, "I'll take my tea in here, please."

"Marianne!" At the sound of Louisa's voice, she spun around in surprise. "My dear, whatever are you wearing?"

Marianne looked down at herself ruefully. "Ah – it is only my father's old overcoat," she replied, smoothing back her hair self-consciously. Several long, tangled dark strands hung about her shoulders. She tugged them back with her numbed fingers.

"My dear, you look a fright," Louisa laughed. It was only then that Marianne realised that Mrs Weston was dressed in her own overcoat.

"Are you going out?" she asked.

"Yes, I'm afraid I must," Louisa replied, walking quickly towards her friend. "And I'm afraid that I need you to promise me something." She looked very worried, and Marianne stopped fussing with her hair to take her hands in her own.

"What is it? Where are you going?"

"I've just had word from the Wilcox farm," said Louisa. "It seems that the night air yesterday did Mrs Wilcox no good. She has taken quite ill today, and Miss Thatcher has begun to feel rather unwell herself. They've asked if I could spend a few days with them, and tend to the children."

"But – haven't they a hired girl to care for them?"

"They do," Louisa replied, releasing Marianne's hands to pull on her gloves. "But she is rather young herself, and can't possibly care for the children and tend the house on her own. And poor Mrs Wilcox and Miss Thatcher could certainly do with my help as well. But my dear – would you look after James and Philip while I am gone?"

"Of course!" Marianne replied. "Have you rung for the carriage?"

"No." Louisa looked down. "I thought I would ride."

"Silly creature!" Marianne scolded. "Of course you must take the carriage, or you'll certainly become ill yourself!" Marianne embraced the small woman. "Do be careful," she said earnestly. "And come back soon."

"I will," Louisa promised. She began to walk towards the door and Marianne followed. "Only please tell Philip where I am gone when he returns home."

Marianne's heart sank unexpectedly. "Captain Weston does not know?" she asked.

"No – I have not seen him since the word came," said Louisa. She fastened her bonnet and embraced her friend once again. "Good-bye! I shall see you very soon. Please kiss James for me."

Marianne mumbled her good-byes, her head suddenly swimming. Then Louisa was gone, and the door closed behind her. Marianne leaned against the wall, suddenly feeling tired and defeated.

"There," she said, almost before she had formed the thought in her mind. "It is done. It is inevitable now." She felt like laughing and crying at once. Instead, she turned and walked slowly back into the library, where she sat by the fire, still dressed in her father's dirty and torn coat, and waited for her solitary meal.

FOURTEEN

Marianne waited for Captain Weston to return home. The sun set over the frosty tree-tops west of Barronsgate, and the house grew dim around the edges of the glow from the hearths and the candle light. She ordered that dinner should be held for Weston, but still he did not come. Finally, she settled in the dining room for a solitary meal of warm soup and cold meat. Though she ate without appetite, she lingered over the repast, almost grimly patient. At last the plates were cleared away, and still she stayed. There came from the hall the sound of a man's boots. Marianne sat upright suddenly, feeling a dizzy flush creep over her skin. She heard his voice, and then she listened as his steps clicked smartly up the stairs. She waited, but he did not come back down. Fatigue washed over her; she suddenly felt as though she could not hold up her head any longer. With effort, she rose from the table and made her way up the same stairs on which Weston had made his escape. Lingering for a moment outside her own bedroom, she listened for sounds from down the hall. She could see the outline of his doorway in the dim passage – his door was closed, and she could discern no sounds from within. Marianne pressed her hot cheek against her own cool door, her fingers grazing the handle. Then, with an effort, she opened her eyes and entered her own dim, solitary chamber. A cheerless little fire was ebbing away in the hearth, and the flame from her candle seemed faint to her eyes. She sat down upon the bed and rang for Sarah.

The kind little maid brushed her mistress's hair in silence, and helped her undress, finally leaving with scarcely a word. Marianne lay back upon the bed gratefully, pulling the covers around her and willing sleep to come. It would not. Instead, the memory of his lips upon hers, the warmth from his body pressed itself into her mind.

She grew restless, thirsty. She had felt almost triumphant afterwards, knowing that it was she who had touched him, pressed her lips upon his. Now she felt anguished as she replayed that moment. *Why did he not hold me, as he did before?* she wondered. The rigidity of his frame, the way his arms remained pressed against his sides taunted her memory. *Was he repulsed by me? Perhaps my actions caused him to remember that what he once did is now repugnant to him!*

Marianne did not realise that she had cried out until she heard the footsteps in the hall, the knock upon the door.

"Miss Reed!" Weston's voice was muffled through the door. "Are you all right?"

"Yes," she replied, her voice barely audible. She cleared her throat and spoke again. "Yes, thank you. It was – a nightmare."

"Good night then," the Captain replied, and then his footsteps padded back down the hall.

Marianne lay back upon her pillows, her heart pounding, the bedsheets clutched so tightly in her hand that her knuckles had turned white. She curled up onto her side, squeezed shut her eyes and waited impatiently for sleep to come.

They did not see each other at all the following day. Weston left early, and Marianne spent the afternoon wandering about the grounds with James' little terrier. That evening, she went to the nursery to play with Louisa's son.

"Captain Weston was here this morning," the nurse told her. "He loves the little one a great deal, I think."

Marianne looked up in surprise. "Indeed," she murmured. She stared at James, who was tugging fixedly at the hem of her dress. All at once, she felt inexplicably rent with pity and desperation. Gently, she freed the child's fingers from her dress. He whimpered, reaching his arms towards her. She lifted him, bestowed a quick kiss on his cheek, then handed him to the nurse and walked swiftly out of the nursery.

She wandered aimlessly about the house, frustrated for the first time in her life at Barronsgate's dignified quiet and stillness. She pulled on her cloak and burst out of the front door, but she did not have the heart to go riding or walking. Instead, she walked around the side of the house to a small garden hedged by low, crumbling walls. Years ago, she knew, it had been a small chapel to serve the religious needs of her ancestors, but it had burnt to the ground long before Marianne was born. The servants tended the ground now with their own vegetables and flowers; when she was a child, Marianne had often played there with Sarah and other servants' children. She came this way seldom now. She doubted that the Westons even knew of its existence.

It was a cold day, and the leaves and vines at her feet were withered and dead. They crunched as she walked through them. She found a low spot in the wall and sat down. A chill crept up around her, up from the crumbling stone and through her clothes. But the place was quiet and peaceful, with a soothing stillness different from the oppressive peace inside the house. She sighed, closing her eyes, listening to the far-off singing of birds.

The sound of a footfall in the secluded garden startled her. She opened her eyes to find the Captain a few feet away from her, surveying the garden with guarded eyes. "You will catch cold," he said.

"Perhaps," Marianne replied, trying to smile easily. "Will you sit and catch cold with me?"

"No, thank you," he replied easily, advancing towards her nonetheless. "I prefer to remain well."

"I have a message from Louisa," said Marianne; with an effort, she kept her voice light and steady. "She had to go away to the Wilcoxes. Mrs Wilcox and her sister are unwell. She has gone to tend the children."

"Yes, I know. The servants told me last night."

Marianne raised her eyebrows in surprise. "And did the servants also tell you where to find me?"

"No." Weston shifted his posture, leaning slightly against a high portion of the wall. "I've come upon you quite by accident. I've never been on this part of the grounds."

"It's a haunt that's mostly left to the servants. They tend it as a garden in the summer. It was once a chapel." Marianne stood then, her limbs stiff from the cold.

"Have I chased you away?" Weston asked lightly, looking off towards the lawn and the other gardens beyond.

"No, I'm a little cold. I think I will find a warm fire." She moved to walk past him. He reached out and caught her arm. She spun in surprise.

"And if I didn't come upon you by accident?" he asked, his voice suddenly tense, almost cruel. He fixed his bright, penetrating eyes upon hers. "What would you say if you knew I was following you?"

"I would ask why, when you have avoided me these two days." Her voice surprised her; it sounded bold and haughty to her ears. She drew herself up to meet his gaze.

"Perhaps I don't trust you. Perhaps I feared for your virtue. Young Paul seems rather taken with his mistress, and I don't perceive that you mind." His eyes were locked with hers, cruel and challenging and gleaming with excitement.

Marianne laughed then, enjoying the way it caused a flicker of frustration to tighten his features. She felt suddenly elated, giddy almost. "Captain Weston! I am used to your tricks! Be as vulgar as you will. I don't care." She pulled away from him, pausing only for a moment, feeling as though she were giving him a chance to react, to move forward, to reach out and grasp her once again. He did not. She turned her back coolly on him and walked away, knowing that he watched her as she did so. She felt like laughing, like turning back and laughing at him. But she did not – she rounded the corner of the house, disappearing from his view. She felt as though a very bright lamp had suddenly been put out when she could no longer feel his gaze upon her.

She knew that she would eat alone once again; she was not wrong. If Weston entered Barronsgate at all that evening, Marianne did not know it. She retired to the library to read quietly by the fire, then stopped by the nursery to kiss James goodnight before she closed herself in her own bedroom. Sarah came once again to unbind Marianne's hair. But Marianne took the comb from her.

"It's all right, Sarah," she said. "I can manage."

She thought the little servant cast her a worried glance before leaving the room. When the door was safely shut, she continued to comb her own hair before the small mirror, enjoying the way the dark waves fell about her smooth, fair skin. She stood in her long nightgown, stoking the fire, watching with pleasure as a warm, gentle glow filled the room. She heard the footsteps in the hall, and she sat down upon the bed. Her body tingled as she waited – she felt, more than heard, the sound of the door handle turning. The door swung gently open, and Captain Weston entered her room silently and she turned to him without surprise. He moved slowly towards the bed, and Marianne watched the firelight play across his handsome face, flicker in his bright, terrifying, alluring eyes. Warm expectation uncurled itself in her stomach as she watched him move across the room towards her, so slowly, so very slowly, she felt. He stopped before her and took her gently by the arms, pulling her up towards him. She wanted to feel the warmth of his body against hers – she was drawn to him, a magnet, a spring pulled against its tight coils. He kissed her, and it was different than it had been the other times. His mouth was at once gentle and impatient. She wound her arms around his torso, her fingers into his hair, wanting to touch all of him at once. He slipped her nightdress over her shoulders, and it fell about her feet. The cool air and his hot gaze swirled over her naked skin, and she enjoyed the feeling. His hands moved across her body, leaving hot, invisible traces everywhere they touched, and she fell so slowly with him onto the bed, her fingers tugging to pull away his shirt. She pressed him against her, loving the heat and the strength of his body. He pushed her away suddenly to look into her face, then pulled her back against himself once again. The sudden, desperate strength of his embrace surprised her.

"Marianne," he said, as though he were testing the sound of her name. "Miss Reed." He kissed her again, more gently this time. And it surprised her that nothing he did after that surprised her.

She awoke early the next morning, before the sun or the servants had yet risen. Weston lay sleeping in her bed, the skin of his arm, his shoulder, his face dark and surprisingly smooth against the sheets. She allowed herself one lingering glance over the contours of his body, then she quickly dressed herself, her back to the bed, leaving off the underclothes whose difficult hooks and laces only Sarah could make sense of, then slipped the key from her dresser into her palm. She left her bedroom, her hair still unbound and tangled about her face, and locked the door behind her. Then she slipped down the hallway and did the same to his bedroom door, and finally, pushed the key back underneath the door where Weston slept. Marianne knew that this would not keep the servants from their suspicions and their guesses, but she also knew that suspicion was better than certainty. She descended quietly to the library, where she tied her hair back as well as she could without a comb or a mirror. The room was cold: the fire had not yet been lit. Before long, however, she could hear the bustle of servants about the house. Lifting her chin and smoothing her skirt, she strode out into the hall.

"'Tis early for you to be up, Miss!" Mrs Frawley exclaimed, emerging from the kitchens.

"I heard Jason barking," Marianne lied easily, meeting the older woman's shrewd eyes.

"Really." The housekeeper shook her head regretfully. "I heard nothing myself. But I'll see that he's not left to roam the grounds at night." She turned to go without waiting to be dismissed. "Will you breakfast now, Miss, or will you wait for the Captain?" she asked over her shoulder.

"No, I won't wait," Marianne replied, turning her own back upon the woman. "I'll take my breakfast in the library," she called over her shoulder as she strode back into that room.

As she stood by the newly built fire, waiting for her meal, Marianne began to grow skittish, and fought the urge to pace before the fire. She pricked her ears for the sound of his boots upon the polished floors. At last the hot chocolate and warm biscuits were brought in, and Marianne took her seat at the small table by the window. She found that despite her nervousness, she was rather hungry. As she ate, she noticed a certain languor to her movements, a warm, delicious, aching fatigue in her limbs. She thought of the Captain, right now in her bed, and could not help but blush, though she wanted to laugh. A warm, excited tingle unfolded in her belly.

At last, just as Marianne was finishing her breakfast, Weston himself appeared in the doorway. Startled, Marianne shot to her feet, almost upsetting the table as she did so. Feeling foolish, she sat down again. "Good morning, Captain Weston," she said, pretending an interest in the scattered crumbs of her meal. "I didn't hear you come down."

"Indeed," he replied impassively, not moving. He flickered his eyes across the room and turned to go.

"Captain," Marianne called, not wanting him to walk away, wanting him to sit down across from her and eat his breakfast and make plans for the day, to talk to her easily, and ask her how she would spend her afternoon. "Have you breakfasted?" she asked, her voice suddenly shrill.

"I'm not hungry," he replied, and with a frosty nod, he turned and strode away down the hall. Marianne listened to the neat click of his footsteps as the approached the front door, then traversed the threshold, then were gone, masked by the closing of the heavy door. The warm tingling in her belly had turned into a dull, heavy coldness. She sat still for a long moment, staring at the doorway where he had stood, then slowly she rose and made her way back to her bedroom.

Though it was still early, Sarah had already been there, and had neatly made the bed and swept away yesterday's dress. Marianne rang for her, then sat silently as she combed and pinned her mistress's hair, then helped her to dress. Then Miss Reed returned to the library, where she spent the morning trying to read one of her father's old books. She ate a solitary meal in the dining room, then returned once again to the library. She felt strangely calm, detached. She sat for a long while in her father's chair by the fire, her book open and unread in her lap, staring out the window. She took her tea there, then called for the nurse to bring her James. She played quietly with the little boy until the nurse shyly suggested that it was past his bedtime. Marianne allowed him to be returned to the nursery, then told the servants not to bother to prepare any dinner for her. Instead, she retired early to her own bedroom.

There, she took a seat at the darkening window and stared down onto the dim, frosty grounds. She heard the sound of the front door closing, then the sound of Weston's boots on the stairs. She heard him walk past her room, and enter his own. Then she heard his footsteps returning towards her room. She stood. He paused before her door; she wondered whether he would knock. One step fell on the polished floor, as though he were turning away. She tilted her chin upward, staring fixedly at the door. Then it swung gently inwards, and he stood there, not entering. Marianne wondered for a moment whether she could turn him away, treat her with the same cold indifference he had offered her that morning. Instead, she stepped forward, and reached out one hand towards him, hating the plaintive, inviting gesture, yet unable to stop her self, to tell him to go. He walked gently towards her and took her hand in his own.

The following day, the Captain avoided Marianne once again, and when they met by accident, he was painfully polite and cool. That afternoon, they had word from Louisa that Mrs Wilcox and her sister were still too unwell to return Mrs Weston to her family for another three nights at least. Marianne herself could not read the note – the sight of Louisa's handwriting caused her chest to contract painfully. She had Sarah relate the contents of the missive to her, then escaped to her bedroom to indulge in bitter tears of repentance. That night, she locked her door against Weston, and lay in her bed, rent by bitter guilt and malice towards Louisa's husband. But when she heard his footsteps outside her door and his gentle knock, she felt moved by a force greater than her loyalty to her friend. She rose from her bed and unlocked the door to let him in.

The next morning, she met the Captain in the hall as she descended for breakfast. He was dressed for a ride, and was headed for the front door.

"Good morning Captain," she said coolly. "Where are you going?"

"I thought I'd ride into the village," he replied, his voice clipped. He moved to walk past her, but she barred his exit.

"Are you going to see your wife, sir?" she asked, her eyes locked accusingly with his.

"I thought I might see how Louisa has been getting on," he said guardedly. His eyes told her that he was ready for her assault.

"I don't believe you," said Marianne flippantly. She had a sudden unrelenting desire to wound him. "Perhaps you are going to see Miss Thatcher. I marked how you admire her when they dined with us."

Weston made a move to walk past her. Desperate, Marianne

called to his back, "Or perhaps you are going to see how Louisa is getting on – perhaps she is getting on rather well with Mr Wilcox!" The Captain stopped short. Marianne's exultation lasted only a second – he spun around, his eyes acid with anger and malice. He caught her by the arm, almost causing her to fall backwards. His grip hurt, but she was too surprised to cry out. "Do not assume, Miss Reed," he whispered, his hardened features only inches from her own, "that Louisa would succumb to such base temptations as a lesser woman might." And with that he released her so suddenly that she did stumble backwards, almost falling onto the banister behind her. Weston himself strode through the door, slamming it behind him. Tears welled up behind Marianne's eyes, but she refused to cry. She balled up her fists and looked around for some item that she might dash to pieces on the ground, but there was nothing. The hall was empty, and she was alone. To her shame and frustration, a sob escaped her, echoing in the tall, lonely room.

Marianne did not retire to her bedroom that evening. She waited in the library, the doors shut securely, until she heard Captain Weston enter the house and climb the stairs. She listened to his footsteps above, then she waited a full half hour after all was silent until she sought out her own bed. She ascended as silently as possible, and locked her door gently behind her. Still, she half expected that he might still find his way to her door and knock softly as he had before. He did not. Marianne fell asleep at last, at once relieved and disappointed.

The following morning, Marianne rose early once again. She dressed hurriedly, and ran down the stairs past the still-dark windows. She rapped upon the door of the servants' hall, and entered. They were seated around the large wooden table, breakfasting.

"Good morning," she said, trying to sound commanding. "I have decided that I will be leaving for Brighton today. I won't be returning. Once I have arrived, I will send for the rest of – what I have left. Please make ready the carriage. I would like to leave as soon as possible." The room was silent, and the eyes of those kind, familiar people who had once been in her father's service, and would tomorrow be in the Westons' were upon her. Marianne paused for a moment, then turned and left them, closing the door behind her. She walked deliberately down the hall and up the stairs to pack her trunks for the journey.

FIFTEEN

Marianne half-hoped, half-feared that Captain Weston would intercept her escape, and although it was nearly ten that morning before the carriage was ready to bear her off to Brighton, she did not see him at all during her last minutes at Barronsgate. She refused to look back at the only home that she had ever known as Paul drove the horses down the lane. Instead, she stared resolutely ahead, pretending not to see Sarah's worried glances.

"I'm sorry that I did not give you a chance to say your good-byes, Sarah," she said at last. "You can come back with Paul when he returns to collect my things."

"Oh – it is good that you are leaving now," Sarah burst out with sudden warmth, then closed her mouth firmly and fixed her eyes upon her lap.

"Indeed," murmured Marianne, gazing pensively at the girl. *Perhaps I have not been as careful as I thought.* She shook her head. *It doesn't matter now. I cannot undo any of what I have done.*

They rode through the neighbourhood in which the Wilcox farm was situated. Marianne's chest constricted with pain and guilt. She bit her lip to keep from calling out to Paul to turn down the lane and stop at their house. *I cannot be so much a hypocrite as to bid Louisa farewell as though I've done nothing to harm her – or James.* Her eyes filled with tears once again, but she refused to give in and cry. Instead, she leaned back and pretended to sleep.

The roads were bad, and the journey to Brighton was a long one. They stopped early that evening at a small inn, where they ate a simple dinner and spent the night. They rose early the following day and were soon on the road once again. As they neared the seaside, Marianne remembered her last visit to her brother, and in her mind the streets of that city grew more grim and dirty, and the grounds of

161

Barronsgate, greener and more inviting. Time and time again, she had to fight back tears. They stopped for an early lunch, but Marianne could not eat. She thought of Barronsgate, and of Brighton, and of the Canadas. *Perhaps I will like it there very much,* she thought resolutely over a cooling and untouched cup of tea. *I do not care for Brighton, and I shall never be able to return to Barronsgate. Perhaps the Canadas will be the best place for me.* And then they were on the road again, and Marianne tried to warm to the idea of life outside of England. All the while, the face and voice of Captain Weston kept invading her thoughts, the gentle insistence of his touch, his voice, the warm scent of his skin. She felt as though she were tied to Barronsgate by a cord that was tightening, suffocating her as she drove further and further away. A thousand times she had to clench her jaw shut to keep from ordering Paul to turn back. She longed to confide in Louisa, to press her lips against the Captain's. She indulged in a fantasy in which she were Mrs Weston, and Louisa, Miss Reed. The thought carried all of her guilt and shame back to the forefront of her mind. *Forgive me, Louisa,* she plead silently. *I did not mean to do you any harm.*

It was cold, damp evening when at last they pulled up before Edmond's narrow home. *My home now, too,* Marianne reminded herself. Wearily, she climbed the steps and rang at the door. Collins was long in coming, and when he answered, it was obvious that she had wakened him.

"Is my brother home?" she asked, stepping into the hall.

"No, Miss," he replied blandly.

"Very well," sighed Marianne, disappointed but not surprised. She thought of Esther O'Donnel with a shudder. "Can my chamber be made ready before too long?"

"Yes, Miss. We will wake Abigail." Collins nodded perfunctorily and led Sarah up the stairs. Marianne found her way to the drawing room and stretched her legs gratefully in the cool darkness. She was not there long before Sarah came to tell her that her room was ready.

"Thank you, Sarah," she said. "I can manage on my own, I think. Get some supper, and then get you to bed. And have Paul and Collins bring up my trunks in the morning."

Sarah nodded gratefully and disappeared to the small servants' quarters. Marianne climbed the narrow stairs, her limbs feeling heavy and thick. Though it was scarcely past her habitual suppertime, she was not hungry, only bone-weary. Once in her room, she unbound her hair, not bothering to comb it, undressed, hearing the fabric around the delicate clasps and buttons tear under her clumsy fingers. Finally, she fell gratefully into bed. Sleep overtook her almost immediately, and it was deep and dreamless.

Marianne dressed carefully the following morning. Sleep and the many miles between her and the Westons had not recovered her spirits, but she was eager to see her brother once again. Her complexion in the mirror was wan, and there was a darkness beneath her eyes. She smiled resolutely, and descended to the dining room.

She was alone at the table. Collins brought in the meal with his customary bland sullenness.

"Will my brother be coming down for breakfast?" she asked.

He paused at the door. "No, Miss," he replied.

"No?" Marianne called to his retreating back. "Collins – why not?" *Please don't let him be with that O'Donnel woman!*

"He is not here," said Collins, turning back into the dining room.

"Where is he?" asked Marianne, though her heart told her the answer already.

"He is gone to Kent, Miss."

"Kent!" Marianne nearly dropped her cup. Hot tea spilled on her hand, but she hardly noticed. "What – to Barronsgate?"

"Yes, Miss." Collins seemed oblivious to his new mistress' shock.

"Why – to see me?"

"I suppose so, Miss."

Marianne sat back in her chair, dumbfounded. "Thank you, Collins," she murmured absently, dismissing him. He left silently, not offering to bring her some small comfort for her shock as Sarah might have done. *Well,* thought Marianne in her dismay. *I suppose I shall wait for him to return. When he realises we have crossed each other, he will surely come straight away.* But she could not help but feel uneasy about leaving Edmond on his own at Barronsgate. Even if he stayed in the village, he would have to stop by Barronsgate to inquire after her. What was it that he had said about Weston? *We did not part friends*. Marianne knew that her brother had a gift for understatement. She stood up, feeling suddenly that she had to return home – *to Barronsgate*, she corrected herself – immediately. She strode out into the hall.

"Collins!" she called sharply. "Sarah."

Sarah emerged from the kitchen. "What is the matter, Miss?" she asked worriedly.

"Have my trunks been brought up yet?"

"No, Miss," said Sarah, curtseying apologetically. "I'm sorry – I will see that they are immediately."

"No, no," Marianne interrupted. "Don't – I must go back." She softened at the surprise in her servant's eyes. "I am sorry, Sarah, but Edmond has gone to Barronsgate, and he and the Captain are … no great friends."

Sarah looked up in alarm. "Yes, Miss. I understand." She bobbed another curtsey and rushed away.

Marianne scarcely had time to climb back to her new bedroom and change into her travelling clothes before Sarah announced that Paul was ready with the carriage. "Already!" said Marianne with surprise. "Thank you – I am ready. We will leave presently."

The journey back to Barronsgate was nearly as quick as it was uncomfortable. Paul kept the horses moving at a brisk pace, and Marianne felt that he managed to find every rut in the road. They stopped only briefly, shortly after noon, and Marianne began to feel that Paul and Sarah were hurrying her along. Sarah kept casting worried glances in her direction and sighing. They were nearly in the neighbourhood of Barronsgate before Marianne realised that Sarah and Paul were under the belief that Edmond had somehow discovered her relationship with Weston, and had gone home to defend her honour! Marianne almost laughed out loud at the absurd image of dear, mild, indolent Edmond actually duelling with Captain Weston! Sobering thoughts, however, checked her laughter. *After all, might he not be angry enough to fight if he were to discover? And if dear Papa were alive? What then?* Marianne's eyes filled with tears at the thought of how deeply this would have wounded her father. *Oh, Papa, forgive me!*

Sarah reached forward and squeezed her mistress's hand sympathetically. "Don't fret Miss," she whispered earnestly. "We are not far off now."

Marianne nodded gratefully, fighting back her tears. She opened the blind enough that she might look out the carriage window. Indeed, the landscape had become familiar to her. Nervousness suddenly gripped her as she realised that she must soon face Louisa and Captain Weston, and find an explanation for her sudden and unannounced departure. She did not know what she could possibly say to either of them. She pictured Louisa's open, childlike face, and knew how difficult it would be to lie to her. *And yet I cannot bear to wound her with the truth!* And Captain Weston – how was she to face him? She closed her eyes, and his face was clear in her mind, as it had been on the morning after he had first come to her. She shivered, remembering how cold and unrecognising he had been – how different from his gentle, warm self the night before! She remembered her own eagerness at seeing him, at the prospect of breakfasting with him, her devastation at his coldness – his cruelty. *Good God!* thought Marianne, clutching her skirts suddenly in her gloved hands, *I am in love with him!* She leaned back hard against the seat, feeling as though she had been dealt a blow to the cheek. Indeed, she lifted her hand to her face and held it there. *How can I love such a man? He is so cruel, so vulgar!* And yet – she realised with a slow, deep pain – *Louisa loves him, and he loves her, I think.* She wanted to cry then, but found that she could not. Instead, she drew the blind firmly down and waited in the growing darkness for the carriage to bear her back to Barronsgate.

It was late when at last they drew up before the familiar walls and windows. Marianne climbed down from the carriage, her limbs stiff and heavy, and found her way into the house. Sarah followed her, yawning.

"Get you to bed, you dear thing," Marianne said with sudden warmth, "only send me Mrs Frawley first."

Sarah nodded gratefully and was off. Marianne slowly pulled off her cloak, her gloves and her bonnet, and stretched out her weary limbs as she waited for the housekeeper. At last, Mrs Frawley appeared, looking as guarded and surly as ever.

"Good evening, Mrs Frawley," said Marianne, attempting to sound at once regal and calm. "Has my brother arrived here yet?"

If the seasoned old housekeeper felt any surprise at the question, her sour features did not betray it. "No, Miss. I've not seen Master Reed."

"Good," replied Marianne, relieved. *He is making no haste in his journey – he will likely arrive tomorrow.* "You will notify me before the Westons when he arrives."

"Yes Miss." Marianne thought she saw the trace of a smile around the woman's lips. She was not amused.

"Please tell the Westons that I am in the library. Are they both at home?"

"No Miss. Mrs Weston is not."

Ah – the Wilcoxes. "Very well. Please tell the Captain then."

Mrs Frawley nodded curtly and strode away. Marianne herself turned to the library, where she was grateful to find a warm fire. As she stood before it, she rubbed her hands together nervously at the prospect of a *tête-à-tête* with Captain Weston. *He shall be nothing to me from now on,* she told herself. *It does not matter what I feel for him, or what has passed between us. After I have taken Edmond safely away from here, I need never see Captain Weston again!*

As she stood, warming herself by the fire, she could not help but pace a little, expecting Weston to appear at the doorway every minute. Long moments passed, and he did not appear. Fatigue began to overcome Marianne. She sat down in her father's chair to wait for the Captain. Sleepiness began to take the place of nervousness, and still he did not appear. She began to doze in her chair, and at last a quiet knock on the door awoke her. She started up, disoriented and suddenly afraid. In the doorway stood Mrs Frawley.

"Well?" asked Marianne, annoyed. "Where is the Captain?"

"He cannot see you tonight, Miss," the impenetrable servant replied. "Perhaps tomorrow."

"Very well," said Marianne ill-naturedly, too tired to argue or to inquire further. Mrs Frawley left, and she rose and stretched. *To bed then.*

She locked her bedroom door behind her, and she was scarcely

166

undressed before she had fallen into a fitful sleep, punctuated by nightmares and unhappy dreams.

The morning had scarcely dawned the following day, and Marianne was awake and dressed. She tied her hair back, and paused long enough before the glass to scowl at her reflection. The circles beneath her eyes had deepened, and her complexion had grown pale and sallow. *Edmond will never succeed in marrying me to a rich Colonel now*, she thought with wan humour. The reflection brought a bitter little smile to her lips.

She descended to the dining room, where she hoped to find the Captain. He was not there. She returned to the hall, and stopped Mrs Frawley, who was bustling by towards the kitchen.

"Has the Captain breakfasted yet?" she asked impatiently.

"No, Miss."

"And the Captain, my brother – he has not yet arrived?"

"No Miss."

Marianne turned away, releasing the housekeeper, and returned to the dining room. Breakfast was brought, but she had little appetite. She wanted to go outside for a little exercise, a final ride upon the grounds, but she did not dare risk missing her brother's arrival, or perhaps the chance to warn Weston. She worried that he was a rash man, and that he had perhaps better not know that Edmond was coming, but she knew that if she could not prevent their meeting, it would be best if Weston were not surprised by Edmond's arrival. And so she wandered impatiently from room to room, waiting in frustrated impatience for one Captain or the other to arrive.

After a time, Marianne wandered up the stairs, and down the hall where the family bedrooms lay. She first went to her father's room, which had scarcely been opened since his death. She entered it now, and sat down upon the bed. Dusty fabric covered most of the furniture, and the room had an unoccupied feel, but Marianne had only to close her eyes to feel that she was a young girl again, and that her father would come in at any moment and kiss her forehead and tell her how lovely she looked. She opened her eyes and drew in a deep breath, willing herself not to cry. *Good-bye Father,* she said silently as she rose and walked out of the room. She walked a short way down the hall to her mother's room – Louisa's room now – and paused there. She wanted to enter, to say good-bye to her mother and to Louisa, but she could not. She knew that the room bore too much of both women, and that if she were to enter, she would be able to hold back her tears no longer. *I need to be strong now*, she told herself. She drew in another deep breath and walked on.

As she descended the stairs, she heard the front door open. She reached the hall just as Weston entered the house. He looked at her with mild surprise. "Good morning Miss Reed," he said, taking off his coat.

"Good morning Captain." Marianne's voice was clear and strong, and she felt as though she were growing in composure. "I am afraid I have some – unusual news. Will you meet me in the library?"

He nodded his assent, and followed her into that room, closing the doors behind him. Marianne walked instinctively to her father's desk, where he had transacted most of his business. She drew a little strength from the spot.

"I have some news," she began, "which may be somewhat … surprising to you. When I arrived at Brighton, I discovered that I had … crossed my brother."

"Indeed." The Captain stood facing her from the other side of the desk. His features were impenetrable, but Marianne could not detect any of the coldness that had rattled her one other morning in this room. He was composed, it was true, and she was unable to read her features, but she did not feel as she had before – as though he were closed to her, indifferent, or antipathetic.

"I am afraid so," she continued in her clear, calm voice. "It seems that he is coming here – to Barronsgate. To see me, I imagine."

"Do you?" the Captain murmured, but he said it so quietly that she did not imagine that he meant her to hear.

"And so of course, I came back. I did not intend to come back." There was a trace of bitterness in her voice, but she forced herself to continue with the same calm clarity with which she had begun. "But I promise you, as soon as I intercept Edmond, we will both return to Brighton. After that, we will trouble you no more. Barronsgate will be free of the Reed family."

There was a long pause, and Marianne was able to study the

BARRONSGATE

Captain's face while he stood silently, studying the top of the desk, considering her news, it seemed. He, too, had slept little the night before, Marianne guessed, for his own complexion was wan, and dark smudges had made their way beneath his eyes. He looked tired, old almost. His hair fell lankly along his sallow cheeks, and Marianne felt suddenly how strongly she loved him. *He has perhaps been pursued by demons of his own*, she thought, *only he has no Brighton to run to.* "I thank you for your kind promise," Weston said at last, turning away from her, towards the window.

Marianne did not know what to say. "Why, yes–" she began. "I–"

"Although you needn't have bothered coming back on Edmond Reed's account. Although you did not inform us of your destination before you left for Brighton, I assure you that Louisa and I were not long in discovering where you had gone. We could have directed your brother back to his new home. If it was indeed you that he came to Barronsgate to seek out." Weston spoke without looking at her, but Marianne sensed a deep bitterness in his tone. She felt at once hurt and defensive. *What – was I to stay and bid you both my farewells after what passed?*

"I did rather regret leaving without speaking to Louisa – but it could not be avoided," she said, her own voice hardening.

"Indeed," the Captain replied, turning back to her. "And have you come now to take your leave of poor Louisa?"

"Well, yes – I had hoped–" she stammered, taken aback.

"Then I am afraid you are too late." The Captain almost spat out his words. His voice was familiar in its peevishness, but his eyes lacked the bright spark that Marianne had come to expect from him in his more querulous moods. "She is gone."

"Gone!" Marianne echoed uncomprehendingly.

"Yes – gone. And so is your brother. You are too late to intercept him, as well."

"I don't understand." Marianne sank down into the chair at the desk, the Captain's words ringing in her ears.

"Edmond came, Louisa was here, but I was not and now he is gone and she is gone with him." Weston looked very tired suddenly, his voice had a ring of defeat, and Marianne had an impulse to comfort him, but she was still too shocked to do much more than

169

repeat what he was saying.

"Both gone!" she parroted, her voice foolish to her own ears, but she could find nothing else to say.

"Yes!" Weston burst out, his voice suddenly angry. "Gone! Both gone!"

"But–" Marianne floundered. "But they must come back! It will be all right. Louisa will come back."

"No," he said, his voice suddenly very small and tired. Marianne's heart ached for him, and for herself – she wished suddenly that she could excite such sadness and anger in him with her departure as Louisa had done. But she hardened herself against such thoughts as she attempted to focus on the present situation.

"Yes," she insisted. "They must come back. She could not leave James, at least."

"She has not left James," Weston replied, his voice frank and level once again. "She has taken him and left with your brother. And she will not come back – not this time. I cannot save her this time."

Marianne drew a sharp breath, understanding at last. She thought of Esther O'Donnel. *He did not know Louisa before she was married! It was during the Westons' marriage that Louisa met my brother!* The realisation brought forth a rush of compassion for Captain Weston. She thought of his unwavering kindness to Louisa, and of his sternness towards his wife that had first elicited Marianne's sympathy for the quiet, little woman. "Edmond – you foolish man!"

She did not realise that she had spoken the words aloud until the Captain spun suddenly away from the window, his eyes flashing with anger. Despite herself, a seed of excitement found its way into Marianne's heart. "Foolish!" he cried, his voice startling her. "Foolish indeed! Do you know what his foolishness has done!" He fell silent once again. Indeed, the entire room had grown so silent that Marianne could hear Jason barking excitedly outside.

Weston looked up suddenly, and Marianne realised that the dog was barking at someone or something outside, at the front of the house. "They are come back!" she whispered.

Weston bolted towards the door.

"Wait!" Marianne cried, running after him. "Captain, Wait!"

170

SIXTEEN

Marianne ran out of the library and into the hall, where she almost collided with Captain Weston. He was quicker than she, and had made it almost to the door before she could leave the library, but he had been intercepted by Mrs Frawley.

"Captain Weston, I am afraid that I cannot offer my services to your family under such conditions," the housekeeper was saying, as her eyes gleamed maliciously.

"Not now," he muttered, and tried to step out of her way. But the housekeeper was a quick, wiry woman, and surprisingly tenacious.

"Do not deceive yourself, sir – a good servant knows what goes on under this roof, and I'll not put up with it. If you won't mind your reputations, then I must mind my own."

Weston was unable to disentangle himself from the housekeeper, but Marianne managed to side-step them both, and burst out onto the frosty walkway. "Louisa!" she gasped. "Edmond!"

The pair had ridden in on horseback, and Edmond helped Louisa to dismount before he turned to face his sister. "Good day, Mary," he said calmly, as though he were greeting a fellow officer at a dinner in Brighton.

"Edmond – whatever it is that you have done, it can be undone," Marianne gasped, "for Louisa's sake."

"For Louisa's sake, it cannot," Edmond replied, taking that woman's hand in his own. For her part, she stood shyly by Edmond's side, her cheeks flushed, and her eyes upon the ground.

"Louisa, please," Marianne appealed. Behind her, she heard the door open, and she knew that Captain Weston now stood behind her. "For James's sake – please!"

"Marianne–" said Louisa shyly, releasing Edmond's hand and stepping forward. "I have done everything for James's sake, even at the expense of the happiness of others – of your happiness, and my own.…" Her voice trailed off, and her eyes sought out her friend's.

"Where is James?" asked Weston, his voice guarded. Marianne turned to look at him. His eyes flashed dangerously, and she placed herself between him and her brother. *Please let there be no violence today*, she prayed silently.

"At the Wilcoxes'," Louisa replied. "We hired a carriage in the village – we were going to travel post to London, but I could not go. We came back, and left James with Mrs Wilcox, and came the rest of the way on Mr Wilcox's horses."

Weston turned his gaze on Edmond. "It would have been better for you to go to London," he said, his voice at once frank and bitter.

"No – oh, no!" Marianne burst out desperately. "You see – nothing's been done that cannot be undone!" And yet in her heart, a small voice whispered jealously, *Yes, yes, why didn't you go to London!*

Strangely, the others seemed to ignore her, as though there were a drama that must be played out, and she was not a part of it.

"I could not go, Philip," Louisa continued softly, her eyes appealing to Captain Weston. "We were going to be married in London, and then come back and beg your forgiveness – but I could not be married without you and Marianne there. Please, Philip. We will make things right now."

"Married!" cried Marianne, incredulous. "Impossible! How–"

"Oh, poor, dear Marianne!" Louisa cried, laughing breathlessly. "I am going to marry your brother. We shall be sisters!"

"But Captain Weston–"

"Is my brother," said Louisa gently, touching Marianne's cheek with her gloved hand.

"Brother!" Marianne felt as though the breath had been knocked from her lungs. She could hardly breathe, could not believe what she heard. "Brother!" She turned to face Weston, who gazed at her with the same coolness that he had shown that morning in the library. Then slowly, he turned and walked into the house. Marianne stared at the door for a moment, then turned back to Louisa and Edmond. She was by his side again, and he had his arm gently about her waist. "Good God!" She understood at last. "James is your son, Edmond."

"I thank you for telling me that, Mary, last month in Brighton, though you did not know it then yourself," Captain Reed replied. "If you hadn't, I may never have been man enough to come and right this wrong."

Marianne could not speak. She shivered in the cool morning.

"Oh, Edmond!" Louisa admonished. "Look at your sister! She has no coat, and we've just given her a terrible shock. Come – let's put her by a warm fire."

The two of them steered Marianne into the house, and sat her by the fire in the sitting room. Edmond sat by his sister while Louisa left to find her brother. She returned before too long and announced cheerfully that Captain Weston had effectively disappeared. "A trick he's played ever since we were children," she confided.

"Edmond, Louisa," Marianne interrupted, her thoughts clearing at last. "Please, explain all this to me."

"Poor Marianne, entirely uninformed," Edmond teased lightly. A dangerous look from his sister warned him that now was not the time for jokes. "I met Captain Weston soon after I joined his regiment, which was training near London at the time. Capital fellow. He and I became great friends – he had a talent for getting me out of the scrapes I managed to find myself in with debtors and the like. I'm afraid I was a dreadful rake and a dandy at the time. Couldn't keep out of trouble for a single day. So when he made a trip to Somersetshire three summers ago, he invited me to come along. And there I met Louisa, and we spoke of getting married, and I'm afraid I didn't behave very well by her. Weston found out, of course, and threatened me with a thrashing if I didn't marry the lovely Miss Weston immediately."

"Only he and I quarrelled, and we did not marry," Louisa interjected shyly, her lashes rimmed with tears and her eyes cast upon the floor.

"No, we didn't," Edmond murmured, taking Louisa's hand in his own. "What a rogue was I!"

"And so you returned to the regiment without Louisa," Marianne continued impatiently, "and Weston returned soon after, and he paid off your debts in London and I know not where else so that he could force you into selling Barronsgate to spite you."

173

"Yes," Edmond replied frankly, without a trace of malice or regret. "You are quite right, I think."

"Oh, Louisa!" Marianne breathed suddenly, turning to her friend. "How you must have hated me when you first came here! Because of my brother, you were forced to pretend to be your own brother's wife!"

"Yes," Louisa confessed, her voice and her face filled with shame. "I did hate you." She looked up earnestly then, her face so very childlike and innocent that Marianne was touched almost to tears. "But not for long – dear Marianne, who could hate you once they know you?"

"Poor, sweet Louisa! You are the kindest soul I have ever met."

"No," replied Louisa, looking down once again. "Philip is. When I found out that I was – going to have a child, he gave up everything for me. Did you know that he resigned his Captaincy last month, so that we would not have to return to his regiment and be found out by those few officers who have met me? He would have pretended to be my husband forever, if Edmond had not come for me."

They were silent for a long moment then, before they began to talk of more trifling things. Soon they moved to the dining room, and ate lunch without Captain Weston. Indeed, they spent a long afternoon together, exchanging pleasantries, and sometimes talking of more serious subjects, and still Weston did not return.

"We will be married in the village tomorrow," Louisa told Marianne as they prepared to retire that evening, their voices almost hoarse after a full day's conversation and confidences.

Marianne embraced her friend, and wished her great happiness, and then Louisa retired, leaving Marianne and Edmond to themselves.

"Edmond," Marianne began after a moment, reassuring herself that Louisa was away in her room and safely out of earshot, "I am very happy that you and Louisa are to be married – after everything that has passed between you."

"Yes," he replied gravely, his eyes deep and soulful; indeed, Marianne had seldom seen his features bathed with such sincerity. Her heart was touched. "She is the best, kindest woman that I have ever known. And I will spend the remainder of my life trying to make up to her all the grief and pain that I have caused her. I do not know how I shall succeed."

"Yes, but Edmond–" Marianne looked down, ashamed for what she was now to ask him. "What of ... Esther O'Donnel?"

"Please, Mary," Edmond whispered, looking up at her with frightened and ashamed eyes. "Please don't ever mention that name to me again! I'm thoroughly ashamed of myself for getting involved with that woman. The day you left Brighton, I severed my connection with her. And don't fret for her sake," he added bitterly. "She is no Louisa Weston. She did not waste any time finding herself another young officer to flatter her and bring her gifts. I wonder whether she hadn't found a replacement for me before I was even prepared to be replaced. I've done a great many things that I'm not proud of, but my wife and my son will give me strength to leave those mistakes far behind me."

"And will you still go to the Canadas?"

"Yes. I've spoken of it to Louisa, and she approves. You know that she isn't comfortable in English society, and she can hardly go back to being a penniless farm girl again."

"Again?" asked Marianne, frowning.

"Yes – didn't you know?" James leaned back in his seat and gazed pensively into the fire. "The Westons were a poor family – farmed the land for a rich landlord in Somersetshire."

"Yes, I suppose Captain Weston did tell me something like that," Marianne said, suddenly remembering the hilltop above Barronsgate, when she and Weston had ridden out together. She hoped her brother could not see her blush.

"Right," he continued, oblivious. "It was Philip Weston that changed their fortunes, first by working himself half to death in the mines, then by joining the militia. Eventually, he came home and bought a small coal mine for his father. But then when I – when Weston left with Louisa, their father would have nothing more to do with them, I'm afraid. Told Weston that he'd have nothing to do with his coal mines and his house if he wouldn't turn Louisa out in the streets." He looked up at Marianne again, his eyes deeply sad and soulful once again. "I've taken everything from that girl – her home, her family, everything. And she still loves me. Have you ever known

175

someone so good and kind and loyal?"

Marianne smiled, and stood to embrace her brother. She felt the urge to cry well up inside her breast. She was happy for her brother and for Louisa, but there was a deep sadness and loneliness inside her, and she suddenly felt that she must be alone. "Good night, Edmond," she said. "Sleep well – you are to be married tomorrow!" And she retired to her own room.

She sat down upon her bed, staring into the dark shadows around her. She wondered whether the Captain would come to her tonight. *After all, he is not married*, she thought. The realisation brought her no joy, and she did not know whether she hoped for his knock at the door, or whether she dreaded it. After all, she could not know what she was to him – was she his Louisa, or his Esther? She waited a long while, afraid and lonely, and he did not come. At last Marianne undressed and lay down upon her bed. She drew in a deep breath, closed her eyes, and hot tears fell from her lashes and onto the pillowcase. She placed her hand over her eyes and cried herself to sleep.

The sky was bright and clear the following day. Marianne and Sarah rushed to Louisa's room right after the noon hour meal to help the bride to dress and prepare for the day ahead. Miss Weston, soon to be Mrs Reed, was dressed in a lovely cream silk and lace gown – one that had belonged to Marianne's own mother. Sarah and Marianne had spent the morning making what little alterations it needed to fit Louisa's tiny figure and to appear less old-fashioned. Edmond had gone in the carriage to fetch James from the Wilcoxes, and that little gentleman fussed and squirmed in his fancy clothes. Sarah fixed Louisa's light-brown hair becomingly around her face, and Marianne handed a piece of exquisite Brussels lace to her friend to use as a veil.

"My mother gave it to me," Marianne explained. "I was to use it on my own wedding day. I'm sure it would give her great pleasure to know that Edmond's bride will use it instead."

"Not instead, Marianne," Louisa corrected gently, "only first. And thank you. But I shall only consider it a loan."

Marianne smiled and did not argue. She helped Louisa finish with her final touches, then she herself dressed in a simple, sky-blue gown from Brighton. Sarah fixed her mistress's hair simply and becomingly about her face, and at last Louisa and Marianne admired themselves in the large, old mirror in Louisa's own room. Marianne was pleased – the bride was beautiful, of course, and radiantly happy, and Marianne was equally pleased with her own reflection. "You are lovely, Louisa," she said, squeezing Miss Weston's lace-gloved hand.

"So are you, Marianne," Louisa replied, beaming happily.

"I only hope I shall not disgrace you or my brother today," Marianne replied.

Soon it was time to go to the church. Louisa stood up, suddenly pale and nervous. "Where are Edmond and Philip?" she asked worriedly. "Fetch them, or we shall all be late!"

"There is no need," Marianne replied soothingly. "They are gone already, and the carriage is back to bring you and James and me. Come now. It is time for you to be married!"

The wedding was a quiet one, lovely in its simplicity. Marianne was the only bridesmaid, and Captain Weston stood stoically next to Edmond – *probably to make sure they are really married*, thought Marianne with a mischievous little smile. The only guests were James, who sat remarkably still and quiet in his nurse's lap, the Wilcoxes and Miss Thatcher, who had learned the truth of Louisa's situation only the day before, when she and Edmond had stopped for their assistance on the way back to Barronsgate. Soon, Edmond and Louisa were man and wife; Marianne cried a little, Mrs Wilcox and Miss Thatcher cried a great deal, and Captain Weston appeared immensely relieved.

The wedding dinner was held at Barronsgate. Louisa and Edmond smiled a great deal, and Louisa blushed a great deal more. The meal was a comfortable and lively one, and the company conversed easily among themselves. It was announced that Captain and Mrs Reed would be off the following day for Brighton.

"And you, Miss Reed?" asked Miss Thatcher in her simple, open manner. "Will you be living with them in Brighton?"

"Oh – no," Marianne replied, looking uncomfortably at her

brother and his wife. "I have a little income of my own, and I think that I shall take Trent Cottage."

"Alone?" asked Captain Weston sharply. Marianne looked at him in surprise; he had been rather silent all day long. In fact, no one seemed to know quite what to say to him that day, and he had said little for himself.

"No – not quite," replied Marianne, sipping her wine and trying to sound nonchalant. "I will be bringing Sarah and Paul with me, of course." She suddenly remembered Weston's cruel accusation about herself and Paul, and fought back a blush of pain and humiliation.

"Just when I was getting used to having those two about my house!" laughed Edmond. "Ah, well – my Louisa will have to help me to hire another Sarah and another Paul."

"You will have a hard time, I assure you," Marianne said warmly. "There are few in this world like them." *And soon they must be my only companions.*

Conversation soon turned to other things, and Marianne was left to brood a little on her own. She watched Captain Weston through her lashes. He seemed rather unhappy for a man who had finally seen his sister honourably married. *He will miss her, I suppose,* she thought, gazing wistfully at Louisa, who was smiling happily at her new husband. The circles had disappeared from under his eyes, and the colour had returned to his handsome features, but his eyes remained brooding and unhappy. Then, all at once, he caught her gaze with his own. Marianne almost dropped her fork, but she dared not look away. He held her eyes for a moment, his gaze dark and challenging. For a moment, she half expected him to begin quarrelling with her, and she suddenly felt both nervous and elevated, excited even. But then his eyes returned to his plate, and if he looked at her again that evening, she did not see.

At last the guests were gone, and the wedded couple retired to Louisa's room. Marianne sat in the drawing room, which still seemed to hold the electricity of the depleted festivities. Her thoughts wandered up the stairs, following Edmond and Louisa on their wedding night, but Marianne shut her eyes tight, as though to shut out the unwanted thoughts with the candle light. A dull ache had settled itself in her chest. Tears pressed themselves just behind her eyelids. But she felt charged, unable to sit still; she rose and paced the room. She almost expected Weston before he entered, and when he did, she turned calmly to meet him.

"You are not tired yet, Miss Reed?" he asked, his voice at once cold and cordial, as though he were greeting a stranger.

"No, not yet," she replied. As he did not speak, she turned to him, her head tilted, and her voice deliberately teasing. "Well, Captain Weston. We are almost brother and sister now. Perhaps it is not so inappropriate now for you to call me Marianne, and I shall call you Philip."

He stood still for a moment, as though he were surveying her, weighing her meaning and her intent. He did not move, and Marianne felt sure then that he was going to come to her, to embrace her, and then they two would go upstairs together. "No," he said at last. "I don't think so, Miss Reed." He still did not move, but the air between them had changed. With difficulty, Marianne smiled a little, feeling defeated and dismissed.

"As you wish, Captain Weston." She walked past him then, her chin held high, sweeping close to him, her skirts brushing his leg as she went. "Good night," she called over her shoulder, and she swept out of the room and up the stairs and away to bed.

The newly wedded couple left early the next morning. Louisa and Marianne cried and embraced a great deal, and even Edmond betrayed some tenderness in bidding his sister good-bye.

"You must never want for anything, Mary," he said earnestly. "If ever you need anything at all, you must write me straight away."

Marianne nodded, the lump in her throat preventing her from speaking.

Weston embraced his sister, causing her to cry fresh tears. Weston and Edmond nodded politely to each other, Marianne embraced James one last time, and then the chaise was off, and Louisa waved to them through the window. Marianne reflected that this was probably the last time that she would see her family's carriage; she could not afford to keep it, and Edmond was going to sell it in Brighton as soon as he had secured passage to the Canadas. Paul was to attend them in Brighton for as long as they stayed there, and then return post-chaise to Barronsgate once the carriage was sold.

"It is cold," Weston said, interrupting Marianne's musings. "Let us go back inside."

"Oh – yes. Thank you." Marianne wiped away the last of her tears with her handkerchief as she walked slowly back into the house. It was a little chilly even inside, as though Louisa, Edmond and James had taken some of the warmth of Barronsgate with them. Marianne shivered and sought out the fire in the library. Instead, however, she wandered towards the window and gazed out into the frosty damp, thinking that she must negotiate for Trent Cottage very soon. For every day that she spent at Barronsgate was another day in the company of a man that she loved, and who did not love her in return.

SEVENTEEN

One bright afternoon, Marianne sat at her father's desk, reading through the papers before her. Her brow wrinkled in concentration, and she almost did not hear Weston's steps in the hall. As he passed the open doorway, however, she looked up suddenly. "Captain!" she called, rushing out after him. She managed to intercept him in the hall before he could escape through the front door.

"Yes?" he asked brusquely, stopping short, without facing her.

"I'm afraid I'm required to seek your assistance," said Marianne stiffly, unwilling to catch his gaze. "It cannot wait."

He nodded curtly and followed her back into the library.

Nearly a fortnight had passed since Louisa's and Edmond's wedding, and Marianne and Captain Weston had managed to avoid each other almost entirely. He escaped frequently for long hours on horseback or into the village, on obscure errands. For her part, she rode out on horseback whenever she knew he was at home, spent long hours in the library with her books, and even began a tentative acquaintance with Mrs Wilcox and Miss Thatcher, whom she found to be kind, sincere and straightforward people. She made no further efforts to resume any kind of personal relationship with Weston; whenever they met, it was under the weight of perfect formality.

Marianne had spent the two weeks following the wedding attempting to negotiate with the owner of Trent Cottage: a businesslike, middle-aged man in London. She found, however, that he was reluctant to take seriously the offers of a young, unmarried gentlewoman. He assumed that she was in possession of more money than she had in fact, and was inclined to make light of her most sincere offers. She was compelled, at last, out of frustration and desperation, to seek out Captain Weston's assistance in the matter.

She offered him her seat at the desk, and showed him the various correspondences that had passed between herself and the man who would be her landlord.

"Yes," Weston murmured, his gaze fixedly upon the papers before him, "you are quite right – the sum he asks for is unreasonable. I will write tomorrow, and repeat your first offer. I do not think he will accept so little an amount, but we will see if he will not bargain in earnest with me."

"Thank you," Marianne replied, blushing. It pained her to have her meagre finances so openly displayed before the Captain, but it could not be helped. She had considered writing to Edmond and asking for his assistance, but the letters from Brighton were so full of Edmond, James, and Louisa, and of their happiness together that she did not wish to intrude with matters of business. Weston was her only recourse.

"Perhaps you may be able to take the house on the first week of March," the Captain continued, his voice gravely conversational. "I suppose that will please you."

"Yes – very much," Marianne replied, but her voice caught. She disguised it with a cough, and turned to face the window. She felt, rather than heard the Captain rise from his chair and approach her. A now-familiar knot of excitement and nervousness uncurled itself in her stomach. She clutched the curtain in the edge of her hand, finding it hard to stand still.

"Do you not want to stay?" he asked, and she could not tell whether he was merely being polite, or perhaps trying to find a way to end the conversation, or perhaps mocking and tormenting her.

"Thank you, Captain," she replied softly, "but I shall intrude on your hospitality no longer than I must."

He took another step towards her then, and she could feel his breath on her neck. She closed her eyes, searching for strength from within herself. Then his hands were on her arms, turning her to face him, and she knew she had no strength to find. He kissed her, and she kissed him back eagerly, desperately, asking no questions, merely accepting the warmth of his mouth on hers, the excitement of his touch on her skin.

"Did you hate me?" she asked the following morning, looking at his face in the sunlight, touching his hair as it lay on the pillow with her fingertips.

"What," he asked, blinking blearily at the light.

"Louisa said that she hated me at first – when you first arrived here. Did you hate me too?"

He rubbed his face, then sat up. She pulled the bed coverings around herself as he fumbled for his trousers. "Yes," he said at last, curtly, as he pulled on his shirt.

"I see," she replied softly. *Do you hate me now?* she wanted to ask, but she could not. "And you bought Barronsgate to spite him, and me – and my father."

"Yes," he said again. He was fully dressed now, and turned to face her. Marianne felt a hot blush of shame creep up from her neck. She looked down, wishing that she could somehow shield herself from his view. "Edmond Reed ruined Louisa," Weston continued, his voice strangely flat. "He ruined every aspect of her life – nothing was spared. Her own father would see her no more, or her friends, she had no hope of marrying anyone else. Of course I hated him, and his rich family." Marianne began to feel cold, she wanted him to stop speaking, but she felt powerless to stop him. "I wanted to ruin every part of his life, and yours. And that is what I set about to do."

A chill took her heart – she actually thought that it had stopped beating. "Stop," she whispered, her voice raw. "Stop!" she said again, her voice clear and shrill now. "Get out!" she cried. "Get out! Get out!"

He looked at her, and his face flickered with something that resembled fear. He did not move for a moment, then turned suddenly away and left the room, shutting the door securely behind him.

Marianne watched him go, and then turned her face into the pillow and cried. Sobs racked her body, leaving her empty and exhausted. Then she got up and locked her door. She dressed, washed her face in the wash basin, and brushed her hair severely, tying it at her neck, letting its heavy length fall down her back. She packed her trunks hurriedly, and left them at the foot of her bed. She left her bedroom, and walked quickly down the hall and to the stairs. To her dismay, she found the Captain standing at the base of them.

She drew a deep breath and walked down, brushing past him as she went.

"Excuse me, Captain Weston," she said coolly, unable to meet his eyes, "but I must be going. I will impose on the hospitality of my friends Mr and Mrs Wilcox for some time, and then I will go to stay with your sister and my brother in Brighton while Edmond negotiates for Trent Cottage for me. You need not trouble yourself any longer on that score."

As he did not respond, she strode towards the door, where she pulled on her cloak and gloves, and fumbled clumsily with her bonnet, fighting back tears as she did so. She placed a hand on the door handle, bidding her home a silent farewell.

"Don't go," he said to her back, his voice hoarse and uncontrolled. Marianne froze, then turned back slowly.

"What?" she said unsteadily, looking at him. His posture was rigid, his eyes downcast, but his features seemed strangely animated. It was then that Marianne noticed that his face looked deathly pale.

"Don't go," he repeated, as unsteady as before. He looked up and his grey eyes were strangely wild and appealing. She felt her own features go red.

"You want me to stay?" she hissed, anger, shame and indignation seething through her. "Stay and be your mistress, while you punish me and my brother every day?"

His eyes locked with hers. His gaze appealed to her, and his cheeks blazed red. She watched as the muscles in his jaw clenched and unclenched – she was almost afraid of him at that moment, and despite her anger and her shame, she felt herself drawn to him, so that she wanted to step forward, and tangle his hair in her fingers, and press her lips to his.... She looked away, her own jaw clenched resolutely.

"Marianne," he said, and his voice was almost a whisper. *I must not look at him,* she thought. "I ask you to stay. Is that not enough?"

At first, Marianne found that she could not speak, nor could she move. At last she drew a breath, drawing back her shoulders as she did. "No," she said. With difficulty, she turned towards the door once again.

"Marianne!" he called, and his voice stopped her – he sounded pained, tormented even. "I love you."

"No," she said again, without turning to face him. *If I look at him I am lost.* "You hate me for what my brother has done. You will say anything if you think that it will hurt me."

"And does it?" he asked. "Marianne, do you love me?" She closed her eyes. "Yes." The word came from her unbidden – she could not lie to him. But still she did not turn around.

"Then stay. Stay and marry me."

Before she was even aware of a desire to cry, tears were rolling down Marianne's cheeks. "You are lying," she said, "I won't believe you," her heart tearing within her chest at his words.

"I am not. Please – stay and marry me." His voice had grown small and lost. He sounded like a child almost. And his voice dropped to a whisper as he said again, "Please."

Marianne could bear her anger and her doubts no more. With a cry, she turned to him, and embraced him, and he kissed her back, murmuring, "Marianne – my Marianne," over and over again.

Dear Louisa and Edmond,

I hope this letter finds you well and happy. All is well here at Barronsgate, as I hope you will find on your last visit before you embark on your journey to the Canadas. I hope that you will find happiness there, though for my part, I shall miss you terribly. I have some news that you may find rather interesting. I have decided not to take Trent Cottage. My husband would find it rather inconvenient to visit me there. He would rather that I remain at his home with him.

You see, my dearest brother and sister, I have married Philip. Edmond, I was so taken with the idea of keeping house for someone that when you would not have me, I was forced to find someone who would. Mostly, however, I pitied poor Philip for the loss of you, dear Louisa, and I thought it best that someone should stay at Barronsgate to ensure that he does not ruin the furniture, and that the servants do not cheat him.

185

He sends his love, and I charge you both to kiss
James for both of us.
   Sincerely,
   Marianne Weston.

"What are you writing, Love?" asked Philip Weston, as he came up behind his wife, and kissed her neck.

"A letter to Louisa and Edmond. I thought it best to tell them that we are married. I hope they are not too disappointed to have missed the wedding," she replied, dripping wax onto the page to seal it.

"Oh – they'll get over their disappointment, I suppose," he said, wrapping his arms around her, drawing her close to him. He kissed her throat and her chin, moving his mouth towards hers.

"Indeed. Though I think it was rather cruel of you not to invite them. The entire wedding was so rushed, I couldn't invite half the people that I wanted to!"

"What!" he said, drawing away from her. His grey eyes flashed in annoyance. "It was you, my dear, who wanted to be married straight away – you said that you didn't care about the Farthingtons and other such folk!"

"But I only said that to please you," said Marianne, widening her eyes innocently. She moved away from him, towards the window. She pulled back the curtain and looked outside to hide her mirth. She cast her gaze across the grounds, already kissed by the first signs of spring. "Had I had my way, there would have been a hundred guests at least!"

"Of course," he snapped peevishly, his eyes glinting dangerously in the reflection on the panes of glass. Marianne turned back to face him, her smile effectively repressed. "And a wedding dinner, and a wedding breakfast, and a hundred tedious people to bore me for two full days."

"Two days!" Marianne cried in mock dismay. "Oh, a week at least! You really haven't the first notion of how a proper society wedding must go off."

"Proper society weddings be damned!" His gaze was almost electric now. Marianne felt a delicious thread of excitement uncurl in her belly. "Good God – if you wanted a proper society husband, you've chosen the wrong man!"

Marianne laughed throatily, and leaned forward, pressing her lips hard upon his. For a moment he resisted, wanting to resolve their quarrel, but after a brief struggle, gave in to her kisses, wrapping his arms around her, almost lifting her off the floor. Marianne broke away, laughing once again. "Do be careful, Captain," she teased. "That is not how one treats a proper society wife!" And she kissed him once again.

"Indeed?" he growled, his mouth still against hers. "Then I fear, Marianne, that you will have to give up any notion of being a good society wife, for you are *my* wife, and I don't intend for either of us to ever behave differently."

"Good," she replied between kisses. "I'm glad."

*

Printed in the United States
1478900007B/34

9 781413 707731